The A Fredrige Genexesta:

"The Libretto Omnium"

By:

Jake Berard

The Adventures of Fredrigo Benetesta:

"The Libretto Omnium"

Copyright 2016 - Jake Berard

All rights reserved

Authored by Jake Berard

Illustrations by James Kittle-Kamp

Title ID: 6455233
ISBN-13: 978-1535543859

- Dedication -

To my ever loving and supportive family,

To Fr. G...may his kind soul rest in peace,

To the true bros of the Class of 2016,

And lastly, to my dearest muse

Toro Rosso, who made the

dream possible.

- Acknowledgements -

I wish to acknowledge some key contributors to this project.

Fr. Gregory Schweers was my faculty advisor on this project and primary editor. Fr. Greg, a native Texan, entered the Our Lady of Dallas seminary in Irving, Texas in 1975 and was ordained to the priesthood in 1981. He is a scholar, theologian and educator of the highest order. Fr. Greg was the head of the English department for multiple decades and currently teaches electives in humanities as well as the honors Senior Renaissance Seminar at Cistercian Preparatory School.

James Kittle-Kamp provided original artwork for the project. James is a freelance artist from Chicago, Illinois. He is a graduate of Savannah College of Art and is trained in sequential art and storyboarding. He has a passion for drawing comics with a tinge of fantasy and horror.

I also would like to recognize the helpful comments and feedback from the Cistercian faculty and men of the class of 2016, particularly Dr. Thomas Pruitt, Mr. Gary Nied, Fr. Anthony Bigney, Mr. Peter J. Saliga, Mrs. Jacyln Greenfield and Mr. Patrick Mehen who have guided me not only throughout this project, but also in my development as a Christian author.

Thank you all so very much.

- The Adventures of Fredrigo Benetesta: "The Libretto Omnium"-

- *Table of Contents* -

Author's Note 7

Prologue 10

Chapter I – Lussuria 18

Chapter II - Gulam 28

Chapter III - Inertia 42

Chapter IV - Avidità 58

Chapter V - Ira 74

Chapter VI – Invidia 92

Chapter VII – Superbia 112

About the Author 129

- *Author's Note* -

This original, creative work was initially inspired by the short stories found in Giovanni Boccaccio's timeless Renaissance masterpiece, *The Decameron.* The framework of my writing, a series of stories told over a significant span of days, was pulled from Boccaccio. Soon after, as I furthered my studies of the Renaissance period, I drew inspiration for my central, scholarly character from Baldassare Castiglione's writings on the ideal Renaissance gentleman, outlined in much detail in his *Book of the Courtier*. But as I began to delve into these Renaissance themes of rebirth and revival, my writing began to evolve from those roots into new spheres of the human condition, which span across ages of mankind, namely, the quest for immortality. There is something very relatable about this pursuit, because it's something that all men yearn for at some point in their lives—to live forever, or to be born to life anew. I approached this universal, distinctly human quest through the lens of my Catholic faith, and the motifs I present in this work, finding the light out of the darkness, breaking down walls, gaining true vision, and defeating ones demons, coincide quite well with this pursuit of spiritual rebirth and revival.

- The Adventures of Fredrigo Benetesta: "The Libretto Omnium"-

Throughout my writing, I make allusions to Galileo, Petrarch, Erasmus, and many other prominent figures of the Renaissance, who joined in that quest to look back into the past to identify the true measure of man, and what that means for humanity's eternal future. And lastly, I conclude this work with substantial allusion to Dante, not only one of the most prominent Catholic writers of the Renaissance, but also of all history and predecessor to Boccaccio. By doing so, I aimed to bring my work full circle, while further solidifying my themes of rebirth, revival, and life eternal. I also saw it rather fitting to set the stories throughout the Octave of Easter during the High Renaissance, as it is a joyous time in Spring of rebirth of old ideas, revival of ancient culture, and resurrection of the body and soul.

Jake

- *The Adventures of Fredrigo Benetesta: "The Libretto Omnium"*-

- *Prologue* -

Twice upon a time once more, a fresh sun of new birth and beginning bathed the Tuscan countryside in the translucent beams of heaven's grace. It was the morn of Easter, and all throughout the land, the ideals of a time once forgotten had become resurrected. This glorious luminescence from on high shone down upon every soul and city, with the ill-fated exception of those within the shaded walls of San Gimignano—for it was they who remained in the darkness.

Looming towers of stone from the previous age cast the city in shadow, while the rustic thicket and steep hillslopes encompassing the gates isolated her from invasion, by man or refined civilization. The men of San Gimignano were great warriors, skilled with horse and bow, and conducted trade in furs and meat alone. Reciprocally, the women of the land served as feudal farmers, toiling in the basic labors of the age. A lone Count had presided over these lands for over a decade, though rarely had he done so peacefully. He was a man of great strength, whose lengthy beard was rivaled only by the greying mane atop his head, stretching beneath his shoulders. A cold hearted man of much disdain, his boundless greed ravaged the wellbeing of his people. His eyes, born blue, tinged green at times, poisoned by the envy of sickened soul. He grew ever more proud with age, and indeed he was rather advanced in years. Many women had kept him company, though such was exceedingly common within his realm. Gianfrancesco, as the Count was called, was rather indifferent about the coming of the Easter, as he was not a man of God; however, he savagely utilized the chance to call for much feasting, music, and indulgence to be held throughout the city for eight days, in order to properly *celebrate* the Octave.

And so, throughout that first Holy Sunday, they beat upon helmet, shield and drum. Dancers trampled along the coarse stone floors in unwieldy rhythm, as the whole host gorged upon endless spreads of blood meats, cheeses, and mead, stretched across the Count's great feasting hall. Euphoric voices of laughter and vulgar revelry echoed beneath the high vaulted walls, and the extravagant tastes and smells of the evening became indistinguishable in their excess. The Count himself took part in such festivities to the fullest, and soon wafted away to crude, drunken bliss.

Outside the city, night had fallen, and the young ears of a weary traveler heard the boisterous uproar from the main road a great distance away. The clamorous hilarity led him up to the wooden latched door of the great hall, where everyone was still in high spirits. Overhead, the darkened clouds of a looming storm

- The Adventures of Fredrigo Benetesta: "The Libretto Omnium"-

began to thunder and slowly drizzle. A squire, warmed by much mead, not only allowed the traveler to enter without question, but also encouraged him to take part in the night's amusement. And so, the traveler, exhausted to the point of collapse, was thrown into the throng of overindulgent, ever increasing chaos.

When the hour leaned much closer towards sunrise than set, the people had at last grown tired from the first night's merriment and staggered back to their homes for a lengthy slumber, as was the custom. At this incredibly late, yet even earlier hour, the traveler was finally able to meet his host, who was sobering by the fire accompanied by only his most recent of wives and closest court.

"My dear good sir," said he politely to the Count, "You host quite the noble gathering, and I believe beyond any doubt that all of your overly esteemed guests enjoyed themselves to their heart's excess."

Slightly taken aback by the eloquence of the traveler before him, a handsome young man whom he had never seen before in his court, the Count demanded of him, "And who are you who stands before me, uninvited on this sacred eveningtide?"

"I have been suited by many names along my journeys, but you, my lord, may call me Fredrigo Benetesta. I am a scholarly man of many books, though I have written none of my own. My travels brought me to Florence, where I was studying at

University, when my studies required I trek to Siena. However, in the darkness of the wood and my own weariness, I lost my guide, and so I found warmth and welcome within your company. I beseech you to let me remain only for the night."

The women of the present gathering took quite a notice in Fredrigo as he was a tall young man with dark hair and fair skin. He was of the highest manners and courtesy, who had come to learn much through his travels of study. He proved a sharp contrast to the other men to which the ladies were accustomed.

"Oh, but let him stay the night," harped the Count's wife with piercing eyes of longing.

"I see no reason why not," gruffly remarked the Count, "He seems a man of much knowledge and value. Tell me, boy, of your travels." And so Fredrigo proceeded to enlighten the Count and his court on his many journeys throughout Europe, which they enjoyed greatly for he was an incredibly gifted teller of tales. They conversed for quite some time, as the minutes melted away in the warmth of the fire before them.

Eventually there came a lull, and the women looked around in search of entertainment, for the players and dancers had gone home far earlier and were undoubtedly slipping into drunken dreams by this hour. There was nothing to be done, until a spark enkindled the wild curiosity of a handmaiden.

"Fredrigo, dear sir, you are with much certainty the finest man of intellect ever to be within these halls. Let us take him to the *Libretto Omnium*." Everyone within the company, besides the honorable guest, jolted as if being lashed by dried leather whips.

"Silence creton! We do not speak of such things," viciously retorted the Count. "Know your place within this court."

"Be calm," soothed the Countess, stroking his hand as she spoke. "Perhaps he can, indeed, reveal to us what is unseen." Anxious whispers exchanged among men were consumed by a sullen silence. Eyes flickered from the scholar to the Count, who sat pondering as if in a far off, troubled dream. The fresh timber soon kindled to ashen dust, and yet still no words had been spoken. The hour had, indeed, grown quite old; however, not a soul present did yawn, as everyone vigilantly awaited the Count's response with straining eyes like owls.

"And so it shall be." The soundless stillness was at last blown asunder by the weighty words of the Count. As if by ritual, all within the great feasting hall solemnly rose to their feet. The last log lay crumbing in a faint glow of dying embers, as the Count and his retinue filed out of the hall. Fredrigo consciously followed, for he was the last of the procession.

The Count lead the company in the shade of night through many great chambers of crude excellence, adorned with iron

- The Adventures of Fredrigo Benetesta: "The Libretto Omnium"-

swords and animal tusks. Fredrigo would not have been impressed by these barbaric rooms in the least, as he had seen the true beauty of the age along his travels. At last, they stood before the immense, gilded frame of a broad mirror. The Count paused to admire what was reflected before him. "What do you see, Fredrigo?" said he in a pensive whisper.

"Not much of anything, as my eyes are clouded in this darkness."

"Soon, you shall see the most magnificent treasures beyond imagination."

"As will you," gently responded the traveler, but the Count was preoccupied and perceived not his guest's mumblings. He tenderly placed his fingertips to the polished glass and delicately nudged the mirror. The reflective surface began to hinge open within the gilded frame. A rusty creak was heard, for the portal had not been opened for quite the span of months and years. Soon there lay a rectangle of blackness, where the glass once stood. Led by torch light, the host stepped through the frame of gold and began descending into a crypt housing even finer riches.

The light of flame within the Count's clutched fist soon began to be refracted by troves of jewels and treasure. A hoard beyond price, such was the spoil of endless plunder. And yet, Fredrigo remained impassive, as the prize of greatest worth within this cache remained locked away. At the end of this elongated tunnel of wealth, a lone beam of moonlight seeped from the surface and fell upon a solitary pedestal. Atop it lay the *Libretto Omnium*, buckled shut.

"Legend tells of a man of supreme wisdom, who lived atop a mountain. He had so conquered the mortal needs of the flesh that he withstood the harsh summit without food, water, rest or nourishment for a decades on end. For, he had unlocked the secrets to surmount the sufferings of life, including death. This is his manuscript. It is said that within it lies the keys to immortality. Every great man of knowledge to lay eyes upon it has been unable to decipher its meaning, as it is written in a dialect far forgotten. Fredrigo… look upon it."

With much awe-struck delicacy, he laid his hands upon the leather-bound manuscript of unspoken value. Running his fingers along the spine, he soon came upon deeply engraved symbols within the leather.

"The private journal of Azreal Salvestro."

He unlatched the manuscript, and in the gasping astonishment of all those present, he began to read.

- *The Adventures of Fredrigo Benetesta: "The Libretto Omnium"*-

- Chapter 1: Lussuria -

And so, he spoke aloud for all to hear.

*   *   *   *   *

XIII Febrarii MCV Anno Domini

I thumped upon the thorn-thatched door of the one they call Celebus. Without much delay he stood before me, worn by many winters, yet stout and resolute in his wisdom. I looked down into the cataracts of a man who had once seen such sin and sorrow, standing before me unbroken and unbent by the weight of longing.

'What brings a young man of such strength to these outskirts?' said he to me in a stern tone. 'If you have lost your way, I have no aid to offer you.'

'Indeed, I have lost my way, sage sir, but not along the path to which you refer. I am Azrael Salvestro, and I seek your council, for it is you who have conquered the passions of the flesh.'

He glared in silence, then spoke. 'You may come inside to tell me of your sent purpose.'

I stepped within the makeshift shed of thorns, twigs, and palm leaves, which sheltered him against the unceasing winds of the wasteland he solely occupied. Certain legends told that he had lived in such a way for forty years—though other tales preached longer. Ancient texts leaned against the wall across from sparse fruits piled in the corner. The place smelled of warm, wild honey. There was no bed to be seen, only a place within the sandy floor which looked condensed after repeated rest upon it. Across the room, stood a lone table with one chair, from which the old man undoubtedly conducted his studies. There, he bid me to sit down, so that I might tell him of my journey. I remember without flaw the words that he spoke:

'Who has sent you to this clandestine place? And for what purpose have you come?'

'I have come so that I may learn to conquer the temptation of the flesh as you have. My master is mine own to know, though I come before you as one along a righteous quest in search of something still unknown to me. However, first among all things, I must master the desirous impurities of my own body, as my flesh is rotting in sin.'

Each of the words I spoke seemed to sourly strike his ears, as if he had not heard the voice of another man in decades.

After much time, he replied in an aged, yet unquivering tone: 'The passions of man's corrupted heart are not easily overcome. You will not find the answers you are searching for here. This shelter has remained unsullied by carnal knowledge, for no other being dwells within ten leagues of the place I rest my head after each sunset. But if you wish to ultimately vanquish such desires, you must travel to six days and nights to the city of *Tentazione*, the land of the lustful. Such was the realm which I fled to pursue a life of mild blessedness. Voglia was the king during the time of my flight, but undoubtedly his son Brama sits atop the throne now. You must enter his adulterated court. There, you shall face true enticement and soon after, your ultimate trial. Go now to do battle with temptation as was destined.'

I left without speaking, internally vowing to one day return to this place with a token of my victory.

XIV Februarii MCV Anno Domini

On the sixth sleepless day, I arrived, hooded, to the twisted iron gates of the place they call Tentazione. A countless horde of birds occupied the main roads and rooftops. Their calls were deafening, and all throughout the day, screeches, clucks, and moans could be heard from every place and sill. As I roamed the city streets in search of the palace of the King, people were bustling around in every which direction. They shuffled in mass, though no words were exchanged among them, as the harsh, fickle wind, ceaselessly slashed across the multitude. They seemed to move, not upon their own accord, but rather by the winds which drove them. The eyes of men constantly flickered like the burning fires within them, as they strode off to their menial occupations. As I was soon told, women, alternatively, had no work to be done during the day; however, come sunset, not a single soul was found on the streets. Regretfully, none of the men ever had any extra money, despite their constant labors.

I found myself walking through a courtyard of much grandeur, outstretched before the palace of the king. The richest roses of deepest vermillion grew within these hallowed gardens. These were the grounds belonging to the Queen alone, though she invited many men to explore it, as it was quite beautiful. In the center of the garden was an enormous fountain of Venus in all her unhidden allure. She was hailed as the patroness of these lands and endless feasting and celebration was thrown in her honor. I paused only but for a moment to admire the craftsmanship of such a statue, but then I recalled my purpose. At last, I came to the doors of the Royal Court.

Enthroned at the end of an elongated hall studded with many riches reclined Brama, accompanied by his many pleasingly gorgeous servants. Two fair maidens fanned him with lush palm leaves, while an additional pair hand-fed him grapes and sweet meats. As I walked through the great columned hall, many ornamental Greek statues in the nude came across my gaze.

I was rather repulsed, as the hall seemed a temple ordained to the flesh rather than a King's palace, yet I continued on until I was in the presence of Brama. He saw me approach and spoke out in a soft, soothing tone, 'Who is it that comes before me?'

'I am called Azreal Salvestro, by friends and foe. I was sent to seek out your court by Celebus.'

'Celebus?' he spouted in shock. Brushing aside his servants, he sat up as to catch a better view of me. 'I have not heard of such a name in decades. He served as a foolish advisor to my father, before he was expelled from the kingdom for preaching such *inhumane* ways.'

'Nevertheless, he has sent me before you.'

'If what you say is true, then you have trekked quite the distance along your journey to my court. Surely even a young man of your strength and stature must be weary from your travels.' I stood glaring through him in silence, attempting to evade his seductive cadence, though his words were true. 'Come with me, fair sir,' he rose and placed a guiding hand on my shoulder, 'and we will give nourishment to your aching flesh.'

I allowed him to lead me through a series of rooms until we came upon the curtain-closed doorway of an even grander hall. He threw aside the drapery to reveal a chamber of incomparable breadth and depth. Euphoric music from far eastern

- The Adventures of Fredrigo Benetesta: "The Libretto Omnium"-

lands overflowed my ears and instantly dulled all other senses. Large fire pots of immeasurable warmth cast the chamber in a glow of deep orange. Shadows flickered across the faces of countless more distorted ancient statues, scattered throughout the room between the innumerable plush, red couches for which the room was designed. Men and women alike writhed like hot snakes entangled upon such furniture, as many of the King's dancers lightly traced their way all throughout the hall to the rhythm of the rousing melodies.

    I began to back away from such lustful chaos, when a maiden dancer roped me by a piece of red lace and poured a hot drink down my throat. Burning my tongue, teeth, and abdomen, such fell juice slowly set my gut ablaze. Without much delay, all sight began to smear in the orange heat. I dizzily buckled, as the music became overwhelmingly discordant within my head. The only other sound I could perceive was that of the king's malicious laugh. I saw figures, human and statue alike, as beasts, hunks of flesh, melting in the tongues of flame. My hand had no feeling, as I covered my face, attempting desperately to reject the sensory assault upon my body.

    Many hands soon converged around me. *The spirit is willing, but the flesh is weak.* Summoning all my strength, I fended off their wanting grasp. Never has such a temptation been laid before me. In a drunken frenzy, I stumbled out of the King's

- The Adventures of Fredrigo Benetesta: "The Libretto Omnium"-

palace and into the cool air of the courtyard, where an even greater enticement awaited.

A moonbeam bathed the fountain of Venus in pure white light. Whether it be by mine faulty eyes or impaired perception, I saw the spout cease to pour, and in its place, sleek veins of red began to crackle throughout the stonework. I saw her eyes ignite to a low flame, as her whole figure fractured in part at the joints and feet, liberating her from the pedestal where she had stood for decades. Mine own veins turned to ice as hers grew alive in fire. Mortared in place, my flesh and bones were unable to move, yet hers became horrifyingly animate. Her stone crafted heels rumbled the ground with each step, and her copperas hair whipped in the whirlwind which swirled around us. Her eyes burned a more passionate red as she approached me, and I struggled with all my waning strength to escape her gaze. Writhing against her consuming allure, I fell to my hands and knees before her, as she was only but two steps away. My head bowed, as streams of sweat poured from every quaking muscle upon the lush garden grass, which I clenched in all my struggling might. These ancient words echoed within my head.

> *If your eye causes you to sin, pluck it out...And if your hand causes you to sin, cut it off... for it is better for you to lose a part of your flesh, than for your whole body to burn in hell.*

With wild eyes I looked down… and pulled out my christened blade, concealed within my robes, and in one fell swoop of wrathful might, I severed the satanic sculpture of pagan stone at her waist. The figure of distorted lustful want crumbled to a heap of lifeless rock upon the lawn.

I rose to my feet, lifted of that fell trance, and climbed upon the stones. I, the victor over the impurities of the flesh, stood steadfast against the now weakening winds. A new light of purity, not burning passion, shall forevermore shine down upon these lands. I took with me a small stone and set out to return to Celebus.

*   *   *   *   *

The slender stream of moonlight seeping into the treasure chamber had waned to the first beams of morning sun, yet those of the Count's court remained captivated by the words Fredrigo had read. At last, the Countess yawned, for the whole host present had, indeed, been up all night. Thus, she drowsily spoke, "Fredrigo, what a magnificent story of wisdom you have read, but I beg you to pause so that we may all receive at least some rest before today's upcoming festivities. I pray you stay but one night longer, as to finish the story you have begun."

"My lady, I am in need to return to my travels, but I see no harm in one day's delay. I shall do as you wish." And thus, the present company retired to their beds, and the scholar was led by a servant to a chamber where he was to rest his head.

- *The Adventures of Fredrigo Benetesta: "The Libretto Omnium"*-

- Chapter 2: Gulam-

The mid-morning sun had begun to tilt toward noon, when a servant aroused Fredrigo from his shallow slumber. While rubbing the sleep from his still dreaming eyes, he was led into a side corridor of many great windows, though they were heavily draped. There, in the shadowed room, a sumptuous late brunch was laid out along the side wall, across from a table, which stretched the length of the hall.

The slowly waking scholar was refreshed by the sweet smells of honeyed hams, blood sausages, and fresh baked breads, but such aromas were soon interrupted by the boisterous entrance of the Count from the far end of the corridor. He strode in with pace, further rustling the unkempt mane of a poor night's rest. The red-tinged eyes of a sleep deprived madman irritably glared throughout the room, though none met his indignant gaze. The Count stomped to his place at the table in silence and waited to be served.

Within a few drawn out, drowsy moments, the entire company of the previous night's telling was gathered at table. Not much was said, for a dreamy haze laid over the meal. Last night, the Count himself, reflecting upon Fredrigo's read words, was unable to easily drift away to restful dreams. For, as he lay beside his wife, a heart pricked by burning guilt panged within him. Many present at the table shared in a similar night's endeavor. However, the light tingle of guilt's ember and a lack of needed rest did not prevent any, save one, from gorging upon the lavish meal.

After the clatter of plates and knives had subsided, the room yet again slipped into an eerie hush. Soon then the Count suppressed his irritable mood and offered to give his guest a tour of the grounds.

"What say you, Fredrigo?"

The scholar, who was courteous beyond all degree, would never deny such an offer. And so, he graciously responded to the inflamed eyes which received him, "Indeed, a very splendid idea, dear Lord."

And so, the Count showed his guest the grounds of his estate. Fredrigo, while upon the walk, did not see much, as there was not much to be seen at all. The estate was littered with barren birches and throngs of thorn bushes. Moreover, the encompassing moat proved greener than the lonesome, scorched grass splotched throughout the crackling ground. There were few shades of color besides the darkened grey of rubble, and more crumbling gravestones could be seen than flowers. Nevertheless, Fredrigo commented upon all such things presented to him with the highest esteem. After much marching, he called out to the Count:

"Sir, if I may… I have traversed quite the distance in the past few weeks, and my legs are quite weary. Is there a place, where I might rest for a while?"

"Of course. Let us rest beneath the tree over there." As they were walking, the worrisome squire came scampering with urgent news about the coming night's arrangements, which required the Count's immediate attention. And so, he turned to his guest saying, "I must return, at once, Fredrigo. I bid you come with me."

"Nay my Lord, I should like to remain here for a while." With a nod, the Count delayed not another moment and set out back towards the citadel. And so, Fredrigo lingered, sitting atop a stump. He reached his nimble fingers into the storm-softened ground beneath him and raised two fistfuls of moist clay. Alone, he mused for quite some time while shaping the earth with his hands, until the sun began to dip beneath the city walls.

After many hours, innumerable shouts and calls began to ring forth from the castle halls, as the Count's court believed their precious scholar to have gone missing. At last, the plump squire returned, rather short of breath, alongside the Count to the place where they had left Fredrigo, and there he remained, unstirred.

"Fr-Fredrigo! Why have you not returned inside? Have you not budged from the place I left you all those hours ago? The night's merriment is about to commence. We must go at once. But wait...what do you hold in your palm?"

The cultured man handed the Count the soft clay sculpture, on which he had been working. It was unlike any statuette he had ever laid eyes on before. It was the figure of a young woman, not clad in armor or jaggedly cut from coarse stone, but rather with the soft, tender features of a mother. She was hooded, with many roses about her garb.

"This is the artistry of an age, of which I have never seen before," mused the Count in solemn awe. "Where have you learned such a craft?"

"In Padua many masters taught me the long-lost ways of bringing life to clay and sculpture. If I had the time, I would teach you as well. Come, let us return, as your company is, no doubt, in much need of you, Count."

And so, in a quiet daze of confused wonder, the squire and Count brought Fredrigo back to the main hall, where the second night of jovial pleasures had already begun. It was Easter Monday, and by this hour, much word had been spread of the Count's celebration of the night before. Thus, an even greater host was present to further revel in the sacred occasion—such was the reason for the squire's anxious call to the Count earlier in

- The Adventures of Fredrigo Benetesta: "The Libretto Omnium"-

the day. However, the Count, being an overly *generous* man, called for an exorbitant increase in quantity of food and drink, so that there would be no chance of any soul not filled to its excessive want.

Fattened lambs were slaughtered by the herd to sustain such gluttonous feasting; and moreover, barrels of grog, mead, and spiced wine rolled continuously through the hall—ingoing full, while exiting bone-dry. The night at hand was beyond any doubt more raucous than the previous night's gaiety. However, a certain few anticipated the feast's end, anxiously awaiting the conclusion of the tale that was to follow. After hours of insatiable jollity, the host began to retire to their dwellings, though many remained sleeping like pigs with bulged bellies upon the hall's stone floor. Without much delay, those eagerly still awake slipped into the crypt, dragging Fredrigo with them, so that he might continue to read the ancient dialogue of the one they call Azreal Salvestro.

And thus the scholar, placing his finger to the ancient text, resumed from where he had left off the previous night.

*   *   *   *   *

XXV Novembris MCV Anno Domini

Compelled by my master, I continued along my quest toward inconceivable, unknown treasure. Legend stored within a millennium-aged manuscript told of the prize which was to await me should my pursuit prove triumphant, though even I, after countless hours of pouring over such parchment pages, did not fully understand its message. The only unquestioned truth which I have attained from such lore, is that only through perfection of mind and body might one, perhaps, reign immortal.

Upon my return to Celebus, I was sent at once to the sunken city of *Grassezza*, so that I may undergo my second test of eternal worthiness. The temptations of faulty flesh had, indeed, been conquered, but now I set out to surmount the even greater desires of the universal body.

I lightly traveled the backwoods of a far forgotten land for a span of days longer than I care to count. Carrying only stretched water skins, two bound books, including this log, and a blessed blade never to leave my side, I slept upon rocks beneath stars and depended on nature alone to supply me the strength and sustenance to trudge toward my ultimate end. At last, I emerged from the woodland laying before my next destined place.

Upon first gaze, I thought myself to have come to the wrong land. For, as I looked out toward the horizon, no grand city was in sight; yet instead, only vast expanses of grasslands laid before me with a distant mount, peculiarly placed within the center of such grassy plains. After much perplexed wandering toward the luring peak amid the waist deep weeds, I finally came across the city of my next destined trial.

At the base of the mount, slunk within the soil, a circular dimple measuring a mile in radius gaped before me. I had not seen such a massive cavity within the ground earlier, for it lay beneath the dense grass line, as if the earth had begun to swallow all within it. Along the rim of the perfectly circular crater, thick, ceaseless flows of mud and muck cascaded down the slick walls of sludge and began to pool in the underbelly of the brown basin. Within the pit of pooling offal wallowed the city of Grassezza.

Amid my awe-struck astonishment of such a sight, I almost failed to notice the fellow man standing along the brim within a stone's throw. I called out to him, though he stirred not, seemingly transfixed upon the scene which lay beneath him. It was only after I closely approached him, that he awoke from his sorrowful trance which held him captive.

'My good sir, is this which lies beneath us not the once grand city of Grassezza?' I asked of him.

Many moments passed before the feeble man's pale, shallow eyes met mine own, and then he spoke in a quivering tone, 'And thus it tragically is.' He seemed to quake as each word escaped his lips, as he was a rather slender young man bound to the terrors beneath him. 'I am the one they call Temperanus, the only man to miraculously escape the swelling mudflows below. I

- The Adventures of Fredrigo Benetesta: "The Libretto Omnium"-

have seen such horrors within the depths of the pit before us. There are men, elders, widows, and children, who know not the doom laid upon them.'

'What is to become of them?' queried I in mounting sympathy.

'They are to perish in the sludge of their own doing, if no one liberates them of a glutton's curse.' He fell to his scrawny knees and peered unswervingly into the mucky abyss, which was soon to become the sludge-sealed grave of a multitude.

'I shall descend into this domain of filth to free these people of their forsaken fate.' Without any further delay to exchange additional words, I prepared for my descent into this hellhole. I lugged a broad log of much length up to the edge of the pouring steep mud slopes. Then, with the might of many oxen, I shoved off with much pace, thus thrusting the hollowed tree trunk over the brink. Rapidly accelerating down the slick slope of surging mud currents, the log swiftly sliced through the globs of scum. And I, riding atop the trunk, was splattered in sludge incessantly all along my descent, as I cut through the slimy air. Soon the slopes decreased in gradient as I came upon the bottom of the bowl. My slide was slowed to a drift, as I came upon the drowning city of Grassezza.

Wading at knee depth through the thickening mire, I saw mud-stained cottages rising above the encroaching slosh, though each was empty. The people of the land had all taken to the newfound river-streets of filth and were merrily wallowing in mud like swine. Each of these people had grown morbidly obese beyond compare. Their bulging bellies could withhold a castle's store of cannon balls and even the brawny back of the stoutest Clydesdale would splinter beneath but one of them. As such, none were able to stand against the surging mudflows, and so, I came to witness thousands rolling helplessly in the swelling pools of muck. I attempted to speak out to them, yet they were unable to respond as their language had been reduced to animalistic grunts, due to the brimming mud within their mouths. They had undoubtedly been served much in life, but now it was they who were to be consumed in death, as they slowly sank in the excesses of overindulgent waste.

Yet amid all of this, they knew no distress or horror, but rather they welcomed the mud, for it was warm and they were content in their filthy floundering. Moreover, they grunted for more, always more, for they knew nothing else. These people did not understand the fate that their bottomless bodily want would bring them, yet I knew well. As the depth of sludgy slime swelled toward my thigh, I searched for some means of liberation.

My eyes frantically flashed in all directions, yet, as the pool ceaselessly rose, no ideas arose within me. My heart began to hasten until, by some unknown intervention, I found myself gazing upon the peak towering above this sludge pit. Though I

- The Adventures of Fredrigo Benetesta: "The Libretto Omnium"-

knew not why, I was drawn to the mount, trusting that atop it, I might bring freedom to the people.

And, thus, I began to climb upstream, against the raging currents of freefalling filth. Never before has any man undertaken such labor. I clung to the slick walls, washed over unendingly in sludge. My caked feet and fingers had no holds to rest or thrust upon, as the mud-melting banks slunk around me. Moreover, as I scaled this slimy escarpment, immeasurable muck poured down upon me, thus blinding my eyes and clinging to my dragging robes. Inch by inch, I grew ever more coated in sludge, and thus progressively heavier, as I carried with me the sinful weight of those wallowing in the muck beneath me. For the ceaseless span of many hours, I restlessly ascended against the cascading torrents until I was beyond exhaustion under the weight and exertion of my task. And yet keeping on, I soon emerged from the oozing pit.

Half way along my ascent toward impending liberation, I then began, without rest, to climb the overshadowing mount, which molded seamlessly to the mud-ridden basin. No longer did I have to withstand the endless sludge slides; yet upon the first moment above the surface, the heated sun baked all the muck upon me into encrusted rock. Bearing such a burden, I scaled the sheer cliff of crumbling stone and fracturing fissures, at quite the expense of sweat and excruciating toil, until I collapsed atop the peak. Though my vision began to fail along with my crumbling outspread body, I scarcely saw the destined means of deliverance.

Wedged within the mount rested an immense boulder measuring a horse length in breadth, yet behind such an impressive stone, spouts of purest liquid slowly seeped from the thin crevice between the mount and rock. I staggered to my trembling feet, approaching the massive stone, and leaned upon it, as I had no mortal strength left within me.

I can do all things through he who strengthens me.

Summoning inhuman might never before known to me, I grappled the stone with trembling arms, broadly opened. My shuddering knees buckled at the weight of mine own body, exceedingly wearied from my agonizing ascent. Yet even still, with the force of four chariots, I wrenched upon the great stone. It soon crackled and began to dislodge, thus opening pressurized spouts of water afresh. Then, with one ultimate pull of godlike strength, the boulder was, at last, thrown aside, quaking the roots of the mount as it thunderously tumbled down the vertical peak, eventually shattering upon the dried grasslands below. Yet, what was to come next would prove even more seismically epic.

A raging deluge of apocalyptic grandeur surged forth from the gaping mouth thrown open. Cleansing waters of crystal clarity rained down from the mount like glorious tears of heaven's pity upon the filthy sinners. The refreshing flows from salvation's river coursed down the peak and purified the city once more. Every morsel of mud within the city from a previous age was washed away, and thus all within these lands were born to life anew. From on high I witnessed the purging of a once indulgent people, now undeservedly liberated of the weight of their transgressions. Such is the way of unwarranted mercy, though it shall fall only upon those who turn toward its cleansing light.

Able to stand no further, I rolled beneath the waterfall of liquid light, so that I too may be bathed in such sanctifying waters. As the hardened mud melted away, my heart was lightened unlike ever before. Laying outstretched beneath this christened cascade, I gazed skyward through the water. And in that moment, I undeniably knew that I had to see this journey through.

*   *   *   *   *

Fredrigo's eyes rose from the text, as he thought it a proper time to conclude his telling, for, indeed, it had yet again grown quite late. As he began to close the manuscript, many anxiously gasped. All present had, indeed, been transfixed by the tales read to them and desired nothing more than to hear their culmination. And so, the Count eagerly blurted, "Dear scholar, I know you are a man of many travels and furthermore, that your studies now call you to Siena, but I plead you to stay within these walls but one more night."

The humble traveler rested the text back atop the moonlit pedestal.

"And so it shall be."

- The Adventures of Fredrigo Benetesta: "The Libretto Omnium"-

- *The Adventures of Fredrigo Benetesta: "The Libretto Omnium"*-

- Chapter III: Inertia -

    The cock's crow had long since passed when a gentle beam of late morning's sun brushed against Fredrigo's tender cheek, arousing him from his pleasant dreams. Tossing aside the rugged bear pelt blanket which had warmed him against these past two frigid nights, he rose to his feet in the center of his temporary room. The slender rays slipping between the iron bars of the sole window faintly illuminated the otherwise darkened dwelling. The room was burrowed within an exterior wall of the castle, and thus was completely framed in cold stone. The rather tight space contained only a sturdy bed with sapling trunk posts and dense pillows alongside a small dresser. The outstretched palms of a still waking Fredrigo could nearly feel the jagged ceiling above and any broad shouldered horse would be hard pressed to fit across. In the night's silent darkness, the resting scholar could hear constant drips splashing upon the stones, though he cared not: it soothed him.

    After some time, Fredrigo went out from his room in search of his host, yet the place was eerily quiet, especially since

- The Adventures of Fredrigo Benetesta: "The Libretto Omnium"-

the traveler had grown accustomed to the disorderly raucous which regularly reverberated throughout these halls. And so, he began cautiously wandering the castle, which he had grown to know rather well. Yet even still, the guest saw not a soul and heard nothing save the shuffling mice within the walls. However, such a silence was soon to be jarringly pierced. Amid his unaccompanied wanderings, Fredrigo accidentally stumbled into a set of crude iron armor displayed along a corridor. A shattering clatter rumbled within the air and echoed throughout the stone halls, as iron brutally collided with the rough floor of rock. And yet despite such a reverberating clang, none were stirred from their prolonged slumbers.

At last, after much fruitless meandering throughout the castle, Fredrigo was roused by the distant aggravated tones of labored snores. He followed such sounds until he found himself at the doors of the great feasting hall. Throwing them open, he was met at once by the disruptive hum of countless more snores rumbling from the large host collapsed on the frigid floor due to the previous night's excessive food and drink. Thus, they were all trapped within drunken dreams of incoherent hilarity. Moreover, Fredrigo was soon overwhelmed by the sickening scent of the decaying remains of the previous night's feast, which lay uncleaned and unfinished despite its exorbitant consumption.

In disgust, he began to leave, yet upon placing a hand along the wall in order to stride over an incapacitated guest, the

- The Adventures of Fredrigo Benetesta: "The Libretto Omnium"-

man of high class and culture came upon something which he had not felt in quite some time. To the Count and barbaric men of the hunt, they thought it to be an ancient six-stringed bow, designed with the purpose of felling many wild game at once; however, it never properly functioned as such. Yet even still, they considered it a spoil of great price and thus hung it within their feasting hall. Nevertheless, Fredrigo knew such strings by their true name, a lyre, and was well versed in such musical arts. His nimble fingers began to strike the aged threads, not purposed for the savaged hunt, but rather for the elevated art of melodies.

The castle thus began humming to a new tune never before heard within San Gimignano. As if magically lifted from some wicked trance, all within the estate were soon stirred from their prolonged slumbers to the warming sound of soft harmonies. The stone walls themselves, once cold, began to resonate to the tone of every note and thus amplified such sweet music for the birds, trees, and heavens to hear. All were soon drawn to the source of such sound, until every soul within these halls found themselves sitting before the feet of Fredrigo in mesmerized wonder. And thus, they remained for some time, as the dripping walls kept tempo, musing to themselves: *Who truly is this man?*

At last, Fredrigo's fingers grew weary and the awakening tunes subsided. A moment passed in silence, as all breathed in the final faint melodies still echoing off the deep stone walls.

- The Adventures of Fredrigo Benetesta: "The Libretto Omnium"-

Evermore entranced by what they had heard, all remained unmoving, except for the Count, who was the first to rise to his feet.

"Never have such sweet tones tempered my aging ears, Fredrigo. Where have you learned to conjure these melodies? And from such a bow?"

"I learned to play the lyre, as it is so called my lord," responded the scholar calmly, "in the city of Verona. Indeed, I would teach you this as well, yet I have not the time as my studies still beckon me to Siena in the morning. If I may ask, what is the hour, as I fear it has already grown rather late?"

"Why it is only just past seven," absent mindedly remarked squire still dreamily entranced in sweet song. "Do you not see the sun rising out the west window?"

"You fool!" Retorted the Count. "That is not the rising sun, but rather its setting! We have dreamt away the all of our waning daylight. Quickly! Preparations must be made, as more of our evening's guests will soon be at hand!"

And so all those who had spent the night upon the Count's feasting hall floor, sleepily staggered home to refresh themselves before tonight's gathering. Moreover, back within the hall, the rotten remains of the previous night of gluttony, were cleared away in order to make sufficient room for a slightly humbler feast, soon to be enjoyed. Within the hour, all was prepared and not a moment too soon, for quite the host was assembled outside the feasting hall, anxiously awaiting the third night of jollity.

A lethargic lull hung over the evening as many remained trapped within their slowly fading dreams. Moreover, the Count and his men refrained from laying but a finger upon the indulgent spread, not because they were still overly satisfied from the previous night's meal (such had not stopped them before), but rather the frightful images of last night's reading haunted their bottomless appetites. After the passing of only a few hours, countless yawns began to cloud the air, and the night was deemed dead. Many concluded this neglectful day of rest and revelry, by sluggishly returning to their homes with hopes of returning to gentle sleep and leisure; however, the few who remained awake but a while longer, retired to the crypt, where they were to hear Fredrigo's third reading from the ancient text of everything.

*　　*　　*　　*　　*

XXI Decembris MCV Anno Domini

My master came to me in a dream. At once, rays of clearest light poured though my clenched eyes as he appeared in powerful glory. I saw not his unknown face, as all was blinded in such radiance, but I heard a voice which could crumble mountains and shake the earth. I recall the words he spoke

- The Adventures of Fredrigo Benetesta: "The Libretto Omnium"-

without error, as each sent tremors through my quivering soul, like wind upon a flickering flame:

'Azrael... you are my servant with whom I am well pleased. Go now to the frigid land of Somnia. There you shall combat the sluggishness of soul. For indeed, your flesh has been cleansed, but your mind and spirit remain still stained by sin.'

In a flash of white heat, all was gone, and I awoke with a racing heart and sweat-drenched brow. The next objective along my journey had been revealed to me, and I took no delay in pursuing my destiny. Heading north toward the land of frozen glaciers and polar winds, I prepared my heart for my next chilling test which had been laid before me.

Within the land where rivers cease to flow and trees are ever barren, I came upon a prancing snow fox. Her fur was silken white beyond perfection, as she lightly carved tracks within the boundless sheets of snow drift. I chased after her for quite some time, until she grew weary and fell asleep beneath a needled pine tree. There, I stained the glistening ground of snowy white with the carnal red of innocent blood. I swiftly slew that pure snow fox and skinned it for her pelt, for my bones had begun to freeze at the joints, and my flesh was cold.

Amid the arctic tundra of blistering winds and incessant snowfall, I came upon a glistening palace of reflective ice. Sculpted entirely of frozen glass, the palace towered over the howling snow-scape. Countless towers stretched so far into the sky, that their crowns could no longer be seen, as they were lost in the blustering blizzard. No walls were present, though steep banks of compacted powder were ramped around the castle on all sides. The palace itself was of purest crystalline ice and was fit for any king across the ages. There I arrived, lightly hooded and draped in silken fur, in desperate hope of warming welcome.

At the door of sheet frozen hoarfrost, I only but flicked the intricate snowflake knocker out of fear of shattering the entire castle. Upon striking the delicate door with my finger, it did not shatter, but rather vibrated like a tuning fork and so too the whole palace, as it rang out in one prolonged note like a tiny frozen bell. The tone was soon stopped as the door opened, and there, standing on the threshold, was a young child with an ash-soiled face.

'Why have you come to this cold, cold place?' She innocently asked as she glared up to me with upturned eyes of iciest blue. She had seen no more years than the amount of scars across her face which numbered eight. Her perhaps once cherubic cheeks were now stained with ashen dust, and she stood before me within this wretched chill only clad in scant rags.

I gently knelt upon one knee beside her and tenderly said, 'Is this palace your home, dear princess? Why do you shiver in such cold, while so scarcely clothed?' Wrapping my soft pelt of

- The Adventures of Fredrigo Benetesta: "The Libretto Omnium"-

pure white around her shoulders, I continued, 'And why are your cheeks smeared with soot?'

She clutched the warm fur around her tightly as a heartfelt smile began to stretch across her face. 'Follow me.' She said, grasping two of my fingers in her miniscule palm, 'And I will show you.'

Thus, the shivering child led me within the palace of frozen splendor. We passed beneath countless chandeliers of icicled glass, magnificent beyond any manmade craftsmanship and crossed through vast corridors of refracted light, giving rise to vast spectrums displayed throughout sheets of prismed ice. With each shallow step I took, I was in great fear of fracturing the perfectly polished floor beneath me; however, it mattered not to her, as she traipsed delicately upon numbed, barefoot toes. While ascending an intricate staircase of crafted snow, I could hear only the faint melodic tones of my own footsteps along the ice. All else was deathly quiet and cold.

Atop the stairs, I was guided toward the heart of the castle, where we came upon a hollow centrum, which descended directly down to the foundation of the palace. Overlooking the edge of this cylindrical duct, my nose, which had been frozen raw and thus immune to all smell, was soon thawed and awoken to the smoke and scent of hickory. At the base of the centrum, hundreds of cubits below, flickered a glowing light.

- The Adventures of Fredrigo Benetesta: "The Libretto Omnium"-

'What is that faint light flashing beneath us, dear child?' I spoke incredulously to her.

'It is the lasting fire which warms my family,' she said amid constant coughs, 'It has been burning for longer than any of us have been alive.'

'Your family? Lead me to them, at once, little one.'

Thus we began to methodically descend the spiral staircase, which looped around the vast chimney, ever growing closer to the thawing flames. At last we came to the base of the frigidly torrid groundwork of the castle. High roaring flames were set ablaze atop the palace's glacial core. At the base of this glowing inferno, a dozen more youthful children came into sight, much like the girl beside me. They were heavily burdened with loads of wood and coal, and their unrelenting coughs muffled the sound of the glowing blaze.

'What are you children doing here?' questioned I in rising concern.

'It is our job to tend the fire. If it goes out, my family will die, yet if it burns too brightly, these walls will melt on top of us,' she said dreamily droning on.

'You do all of this work on your own?'

'There is one who helps us, but I do not see him here now.'

- The Adventures of Fredrigo Benetesta: "The Libretto Omnium"-

'Why do you burden yourselves so?'

'For my family.'

'Aye, but where is your family?!'

Her frosted blue eyes grew wide at my mounting angst. In silence, she nodded toward a heap of thoroughly bundled bodies lying motionless around the fire—a truly gruesome sight to behold.

'Oh child, my heart fills with pity—'

'—What do you mean? Go speak to them.'

'Speak to them? Are they not dead?'

'Why of course not,' she giggled, 'they are only but trying to stay warm.' I remained still in utterly perplexed silence. 'Come, let me take you to my father.' The soot-stained girl led me to an unmoving cocoon of wild pelts reclining on a cushion before the glorious heat. 'Father,' sweetly said she, 'we have guest.'

A repulsive, grey head came out of the bundle of blankets. The man had incredibly long hair on both his scalp and face as if he had neglected his appearance for his entire existence. He spoke in a yawning draw, 'Why have you awaken me from my slumber? Surly it is not time to eat. And who is it that comes before me?'

'I am Azrael Salvestro. Is this the palace of Somnia?'

'Beyond any doubt it is. But why—'

'—Answer me this first, you wretched swine. Are you, indeed, the father of this child?'

'Why yes, and—'

'Then why do you recline in idle leisure, while these children and your own toil ceaselessly for your benefit? Furthermore,' I grew in rage with the flames ever flaring behind me, 'why are you draped in such fine linen of heavy exotic furs, while your daughter traipses around in thin rags with nothing to warm her frostbitten toes? Spare me your words. For truly Satan does find work for idle hands!'

Leaving him to slink back into his wretched swaddling, I turned to see a muscular man standing before me, he too peppered in ash, save his honest eyes.

'Azrael, you have done well to chastise our king,' he said humbly to me.

'That is your king?' I scoffed.

'Aye, and these are his children.'

'Then who are you who approaches me?'

'I am Dilegenza, and it is I who have been tasked to keep the hearth. Once, I laid upon the ice like a lug, but now I give aid to this neglected children.'

'Then where have they all gone?' I sternly questioned. He whirled around with frantic eyes, but, indeed, the children were nowhere to be found.

* * * * *

Fredrigo halted his reading as he was disturbed by a rising swell of yawns coming from those present. "Shall I stop at once?" he irritably asked, "for if I bring you boredom, just speak and I will be on my way."

Startled by these cutting words, the Count's nodding head was jolted upright, then he spoke, "No Fredrigo, we bid you continue, for the good of us all."

"Indeed for the good of you all," he muttered beneath his breath, then he returned to the text:

* * * * *

There was a ferocious crack and rumble as if the Earth had split. Dislodged icicles began showering down like a rain of knives, as the raging fire licked ever higher.

'What is this?' I shouted through the quaking and shattering of ice.

- The Adventures of Fredrigo Benetesta: "The Libretto Omnium"-

'It's the children!' yelled back Diligenza, bracing himself against a bank of frozen sleet, 'They have hid out of fear and now the flames grow too large! Look with your own eyes!' The ageless chilled core of the castle had grown brittle and snapped beneath the heat. Fissures were soon climbing all throughout the intricate ice around us, as hunks of sculpted snow came crashing down upon us like mammoth hail stones.

'We must abandon this place at once! Find the children, and I will take to those lying about.' I rushed amid crumbling ice-quake to the unstirring bundle withholding the king. 'Man, get up and lead your people out of this frozen hell!' With the keen edge of my christened blade, I slashed open his swaddling to reveal a gruesome sight. I saw the skinny bones of one who had grown so weak from sloth and sickness. He hissed violently toward me like one savagely ripped from deep dreams, then refused to move, except to pull his wrappings back around him. 'Thus you and your people shall forever sleep foul king, entombed within eternal ice and flame.' *The desire of the slothful killeth him; for his hands refuse to labor.* Just then, a falling shard of ice grazed my shoulder, spiking straight into the crackling floor, and I hurried, at once, to the melting stairs.

As I raced up the slowly liquefying spiral staircase, I saw Diligenza with all of the children ascending too, only but a few lengths above me. The castle of sculpted frozen glass was now of sweating ice, glowing orange. As I ascended the heightened

- The Adventures of Fredrigo Benetesta: "The Libretto Omnium"-

chimney, so too did the flaring tongues of fire alongside me. The ravaging flames, now unchecked, began sweltering the once grand walls and fine ornaments. The palace began weeping steams of melted ice into the fire, but countless more tears would be needed to slake such a blaze.

The steps began to slosh beneath me as I was but an arrow's shot away from the top. Here, I caught up to the young company ahead of me, who had grown beyond weary. By this time, the burning fingers of flame had begun to warm the vaulted ceilings, and soon they were to collapse upon us. Upon our shoulders, Diligenza and I carried a half dozen young ones each as we rushed atop the stairs and toward the nearest gateway to the safety of the outside tundra.

From the first dripping window, we flung ourselves out of that scorching icehouse, only to land softly upon the gloriously well received powder outside the castle. From there we watched speechlessly as the once icy emblem of snow-sculpted beauty savagely thawed and collapsed upon itself at the hands of raging flame. When all was finished, the melted waters and howling arctic winds extinguished the inferno; yet now, nothing of grandeur remains amid such tundra.

'There is shelter but a league from here. Will you come with us, Azreal?' asked the noble Diligenza, as many sets of tiny eyes pitifully fell upon me.

- The Adventures of Fredrigo Benetesta: "The Libretto Omnium"-

'I will travel with you until these children find shelter and warmth, but there you must care for them, as the call of my destiny ever beckons.'

*   *   *   *   *

At last, Fredrigo concluded his third, and what he thought to be his final, tale. He rubbed his dreamy eyes, for indeed, he was quite tired.

"Let us all return to sleep now, as I have a rather long morning of travel to come." As he began to push past the gathered company, still entranced by his read words, none but the squire halted him.

"Sir, if I may," he stuttered as if trying to find the right words, "Would you but stay one night longer, if it be at your convenience, as we long to her the conclusion of these grand tales, which you have begun to impart upon us."

With a feigned sigh of reluctance he spoke, "So you wish it good sir, and so shall it be once more."

- The Adventures of Fredrigo Benetesta: "The Libretto Omnium"-

- *The Adventures of Fredrigo Benetesta: "The Libretto Omnium"*-

- Chapter IV: Avidità -

This morning, the forth gracious morn of Easter, Fredrigo was awoken by neither warm sun nor squire, but rather by the reverberating echos of blasting horns. Thrown from his restful doze, the scholar sat upright in a dreaming, befuddled haze, as the resounding blare was heard anew from his tight window. High pitched voices of excitement were soon heard down below, "The men! The men have returned!"

By the thrid horn blast, Fredrigo had scampered down the stone stairs to investigate the commotion coming from outside the castle walls. At the front gate, he came upon the Count wearing a wrought iron crown, draped in his finest robes. His eyes were ever more enflamed from yet another night of futile rest. The drooping beneath his lashes had begun to gradually consume his entire face in wilting angst. Yet despite his apparent deprivation of wholesome sleep, he stood ceremoniously before the gates.

Fredrigo inquired of him at once, "My lord, what is the means of such uproar?"

"Our armies have returned from the mid-western lands, good sir, and look what spoils they carry!"

"I see no treasures of great price."

"Ha," he snorted, "Alas, you have no sense of worth."

At last, the vast host came before the gates. Rank upon rank of brutish, bearded men began parading throughout the city with their shouldered plunder. Clad in blackened crude armor, some blew upon massive horns of hallowed tusk, while others marched barefoot, robed in rustic hides and dragging dense maces behind them. Soon after, a hulking man of Herculean stature strode forward. His dark flows of hair were only to be outdone by the dim depth of his eyes. A two-pronged scar scratched from his left brow to cheek. Upon the field of battle there was no equal; however, such was the extent of his worth and merit.

"General Forza," boomed the Count, "tell me of your conquest."

"Aye my lord," he spoke with a robust tone reverberating from his broad chest cavity, "They clung to their books and scrolls and were no match to our heavy blades. We brought back everything of value within those trifling lands."

In that moment, a tremendous clamor erupted among the men who had been marching. A large hoard began gathering

- The Adventures of Fredrigo Benetesta: "The Libretto Omnium"-

amid many violent shouts and brimming rage. Then, the men began beating one another with fist and club as their spoils clattered to the ground, and soon many villagers began immerging from the mass with the chalices and other pieces of great worth and began scurrying home to hide them.

"What's happening?" confusedly ask Fredrigo.

"The men fight once more over how the treasures should be distributed among them," angrily observed the Count. "This must cease at once!"

After much effort, Forza was, at last, able to pacify his men, but only after countless more bruises and blackened eyes. When all had subsided, many men still looked greedily upon the wealth of another and much had been stolen by the avaricious people amid the clash.

"Come, let us set aside our quarrels, for indeed, much celebration should be called for to revel in our conquest and plunder."

And so the army and the townsfolk alike were funneled into the great hall where they began to celebrate all throughout the day amid their newfound treasure, heaped in the center of the hall. These mighty men pulled much food and drink to themselves, enough to feed nations, yet they called for endless more. The Count and his court, on the other hand, abstained

- The Adventures of Fredrigo Benetesta: "The Libretto Omnium"-

entirely, as they no longer had any desire to gorge themselves due to fear and wretched dreams.

Amidst the barbaric celebration, Fredrigo could find no one with which to have meaningful conversation, and so he sat alone upon a stool, lost within his own thoughts. His left hand, resting atop a chalice of grapes, plucked but a few and crushed them within his able clutch. Afterwards, he took two fingers of his right hand and, dabbing them in the juice pooling in his opposite palm, thus began tracing sleek lines on the jagged stone wall. After a few additional lines and minor contouring, a brilliant image of a cherubic child dripped in purple pigment on the wall. Such a masterful piece of art went unnoticed for quite some time until the drunken general stumbled upon it at the night's ending.

"What is this which adorns these walls?"

The Count, who had been walking alongside General Forza, lightheartedly remarked, "Why that is the work of Fredrigo, our scholarly guest," not at all surprised at what he saw, yet nonetheless awe-struck at such soft lines, the Count then asked, "From what distant place along your lengthy travels have you learned such an art?"

"I was taught such skills of drafting and paint from the finest masters in Florence."

"Indeed you have," said he still marveling, "My kind guest, we all eagerly await tonight's reading. Forza, I bid you come with us as there is much to be learned."

And so the mighty general accompanied the Count and his closest court for what was to be the latest telling of immortal teaching. Thus, Fredrigo read aloud once more for all those present within the crypt of great wealth.

*   *   *   *   *

XXXI Decembris MCV Anno Domini

Traveling south from the land of everlasting icefall, I slowly came to a faintly warmer region of frost-crusted meadows. Looking down toward the brittle layer of sheeted snow, crunching beneath each boot-step, a lonely flower of vibrant lavender caught my gaze. It was incredibly miniscule and fit perfectly atop the tip of my curled finger, yet it proved the deepest contrast to the consuming spans of white stretching in every which direction. This floral speck was the only piece of natural beauty I had seen since entering these wastelands of tundra. It called to mind memories of even greater beauty brought forth by a higher power, and reminded me of a time before this journey, when I enjoyed such simple splendors—a time, when I sang alongside my fellow brothers and passed the hours in peaceful self-reflection deep within the countryside. Such a passive, pious life was left far in my past, though never did I shed that claiming mantle. Just then, a warm wind blew across my frosted cheeks and took with it the tiny flower, like a leaf dropped in a flowing river. Without hesitation, I followed the course of the breeze as I trusted such true winds would not lead me astray, and they warmed me as I traveled along the steam.

For many days on end the winds coursed unswervingly through forest, meadows, and plains, as did I without rest. At last, I came upon the place where the flows of guiding breeze had been leading toward. I stood before the mouth of a gaping cave vast enough to swallow cities. The winds were unceasingly drawn into such a cavernous mouth as if an immense giant was swiftly filling his lungs. A path of crushed stone descending into the unlighted cave of inconceivable dimension was laid before me. I knew without any such doubt that the next of my trials awaited me within the blackness of this consuming cave.

Igniting the tip of a sapling trunk wrapped in cloth from my own torn tunic, I descended into this yawning void of terrifying uncertainty. Only but a few steps beyond the final licks of sunlight, I was struck with the distant, echoing moans of men in agony. Abandoning all fear and judgment, I rushed through the labyrinth of caverns toward such tormented pleas for help at such speed where my own torchlight almost became extinguished. I remembered not the path I took, nor did I have any means of finding my way out, yet in that moment, it mattered not, as I soon came upon those who wailed in the darkness.

- The Adventures of Fredrigo Benetesta: "The Libretto Omnium"-

Crawling upon the cavern floor by the dozen, a hoard of elderly men and women moaned in suffering. They cringingly shielded their eyes and burst out into groans afresh at the presence of my enkindled torch. They appeared savagely malnourished as they feebly clawed at one another with dirty fingernails. None of them were clothed or had any such possessions. Just then, a soft voice rose above the moans dimly echoing throughout the chamber.

'Sir, I bid you put your light out at once.'

Swiveling toward the voice which met me, my slowly aging eyes fell upon a young woman clad in a tattered garment of white, though her beauty far transcended her simple garb. Her eyes of crystalline sapphire provided an unimpaired view into her purest heart. Startled by the presence and beauty of such a woman, I obeyed her request without any delay and smothered the flame within my cloak.

'Why have you wandered into this place of darkness?' She asked in a perplexed yet rather concerned tone. 'There are horrors here which you do not wish to know.'

'Such horrors are why I have come.'

'You speak foolishly. I earnestly bid you to head back whence you came as I have many to tend to.' After she had spoken, I began to look amid the newfound consuming darkness

- The Adventures of Fredrigo Benetesta: "The Libretto Omnium"-

and was soon astounded to see innumerable faint glimmers of refracted light studded all throughout the surrounding cavern like stars amid the firmament.

'Wait!' I spurted toward her, 'what is this place beneath the earth which glimmers of starlight? And who are you, who lingers in such a place?'

'I am Cara, and this is the place they call *Ghiotto*, the hive of consuming want. Men by the legion have traveled here to slake their intemperance, yet none grow satisfied. Thus, here, they shall forever remain.'

Within the faint glow of glittering light, I saw her shadowy outline begin to kneel and give darkened hunks of bread to the aged host along the ground. Their moans began muffled due to the cave-dampened bread entering their maws.

I crouched beside her, though she never paused from her charitable works. 'You say such men have come in great amounts, yet I only faintly see but fifty amassed about the ground. If they have indeed not left, where do all the others reside?'

'At this moment they burrow deep within these walls and have done such since their arrival—each to their own hole. The countless glimmers which you see are only but the surface of immense troves of precious stones and metals beyond any price, which stretch for leagues toward the Earth's center. They possess limitless wealth, yet delve ever deeper into the world's corrupted core. They have stripped the elderly of all they have, yet soon with age it is they who will take upon such sorrow. Never do they come to enjoy in their wealth, as it matters not to them, nor do they ever consider resurfacing as they desire no more than what lies further within the dirt. In their hearts, the immense treasure they possess is only but a lonesome tear in the ocean, and never will such thirsting hearts be slaked. They speak not to one another; and furthermore, they rebury what has been unearthed for fear of thievery. They no doubt hear the very words we speak now, as whispers echo deep within these tunnels. Such is the life of those engrossed by wanton greed.'

In the moment she had finished speaking, the speckled darkness which encompassed them was sliced by a sleek beam of moonlight, which reflected off the innumerable precious stones jutting from the cavern's walls and illuminated the once darkened space in pale silver light. The ray of purest radiance traced back to a thin crackled vein within the ceiling and cascaded directly into a magnificent reflecting pool at the center of the atrium. Never before had I noticed this pool of such beauty amid the darkness, yet bathed in the moon's beam, it shone clear like drinkable starlight.

Astounded beyond compare, my eyes stretched wide as I disbelievingly asked of Cara, 'Maiden, how does any streak of the night's glow seep into this place so far beneath the surface?'

'No… no it cannot be,' said she while frightfully backing away from the beam after each shallow breath. 'You must go at once, lest you shall undergo the test.'

Just then, the moans of the abandoned elderly ceased. Drawn like flies to flame, they began crawling with unblinking eyes toward the light and the pool into which it flowed like a waterfall from heaven.

'We must stop them!' she cried. 'They know not what they do!' yet I knew not what she meant. Running toward the moonlit pool, she tried to halt all of those for whom she had selflessly cared, yet her many shouts were only met with angered groans and scratches. I snatched her arms and held her tight, demanding an explanation for such happenings. Many more shouts and cries came forth before the sorrowful truth escaped her lips.

'It's the millennial moon! Legend tells that once every thousand years, the first New Year's moon would light the way to the treasure hoard of Rovina Dell'uomo. Elders have debated for centuries as to what lies within such a legendary store, but it is said that it is to be of dazzling worth beyond any comprehension, and all who look upon it become unalterably transfixed.'

- The Adventures of Fredrigo Benetesta: "The Libretto Omnium"-

There was a sudden splash. The abandoned elderly began to tumble into the illuminated, cobalt pool. At once we ran to stop such horror, but they were large in number and all unswervingly possessed by their sole, corrupted purpose of following the prophesized light, regardless of where it led. Unable to swim in their age and sickness, each drowned without exception in the motionless waters along their pursuit of riches beyond man's imagination.

Cara shrieked in terror, as she hid her eyes from gazing down into the translucent water of unknown depth. 'Such are the hearts of men,' she said as a lone tear dragged toward her cheek. 'They recognize not their own reflection, but only see what their corrupted heart's desire.' Just then the walls began to rumble.

A countless hoard of forgotten men burst forth from hidden holes all throughout the expansive cavern. As they rushed toward the treacherous beam of lunar glare, I saw only but the reflection of their ravenous eyes out of the darkness from which they came. The cavern floor quaked as rock dislodged from the ceiling upon each of the host's storming strides. Standing at the edge of the pool, I braced myself for what was rapidly approaching.

The army of men smashed into me at full strength, as I was the only object between their greedy hearts and what they had ever longed for; and yet, I, too, was the only safeguard

- The Adventures of Fredrigo Benetesta: "The Libretto Omnium"-

against their certain ruin. Thrusting with the might equal to the hundreds who pushed against me, I was locked in standstill struggle for only but a few moments, until the ground crumbled beneath my heels, and I was rammed headlong into the moonlit pool. All those who had once burrowed in the darkness soon followed.

The water was neither warm nor chilled, and though men tumbled endlessly into the pool, it did not stir. I could hear not a thing and felt even less. It was like being suspended in light. I clenched my eyes against the temptation which lay at the bottom of such depths; and yet, wild desires began to flood my heart. I longed for nothing more than to see the ageless treasure of legend beneath me. As I sank, my spirit battled the curiosity of the flesh, until my clamped eyelids became overwhelmed by a golden glow, and thus, they slowly raised.

What I then saw cannot be described by words of the mortal tongue. Gems and jewels of purest starlight came into my gaze amid gold brighter than the sun's surface. This was a trove without price and one of which no amount of blood could ever purchase. Transfixed unlike ever before, I sank in a motionless trance toward such riches.

Though I was the first to be thrust into these glowing waters, others soon began to sink faster than I. The host of men, once from the darkness, now made visible in the moonlit pool, were short, scruffy, and clad in their finest armor and ornaments of silver and gold. Thus, they sank like lead. As they descended past me, I saw the souls of those who would become forever encased in the riches which they bore. For though they sank for countless moments, never did they seem to come ever any closer to what they sought. If they ever were to reach such possessions of earthly worth, it would only be in death. Thus, their drowned bodies would lay next to such treasure, but never would they ever be able to embrace the bounty for which they sacrificed their life.

Witnessing this terror snapped me of my desirous trance. Recalled, at once, to my desperate need of air, I began ferociously swimming upstream of the moon's down pouring light. A great fear overtook me, for I had sank to an immeasurable depth in my daze and was thus far from the redemptive surface. As I swam, the countless many, who could not save themselves due to the opulent weight which they carried and were unwilling to part with, sunk past and desperately latched on to me. One by one I struggled to break free from these lost souls, yet they dragged me only deeper within the carnivorous pool. At last, I liberated myself from their hooked fingers as the final few sank past me toward their deserved deaths. I continued to kick upward through the water, but my muscles grew weary and lungs screamed for breath. The moon slowly grew closer, yet I was still hopelessly far away. The beam

- The Adventures of Fredrigo Benetesta: "The Libretto Omnium"-

which comes only but once per millennium began to wane through the cavern ceiling; and soon, all returned to darkness.

When I woke, I was lying beside the blackened pool, heaving water from my lungs as Cara stood beside me, drying her hair. 'Rest here a while, Azrael,' she said tenderly. 'When you have regained your strength I will lead you out of this place, for now all those for whom I once cared have all perished, and you have other journeys which call to you.'

And there I lied, peering up at the twinkling stones within the cave, vowing never again to be consumed by such petty treasures, for I knew a trove of endless more wealth awaited me.

* * * * *

And thus Fredrigo brought an end to his nightly reading, for he had grown rather tired and his eyes began to wander from fatigue. Upon delicately closing the ancient text once more, he was at once stopped by the general who had grown particularly anxious throughout such a story, as did many others present.

"Good sir," the sobered General Forza interjected with beaded sweat upon his brow, "would you kindly continue your reading from this text of eternal wisdom, as I impatiently long to hear how such a book shall come to conclusion."

- The Adventures of Fredrigo Benetesta: "The Libretto Omnium"-

"I am afraid such secrets will remained buried," said cunning Fredrigo in a feigned tone of sorrow, "as I am weary, and must depart come the sun's rising."

"I plead that you should stay beyond this daybreak and unto the next, as there is still much to be learned of the path to immortality."

"For your sake, dear general, I shall remain."

As all retired to their bed chambers, so too did the mighty general briskly stride to his war tent pitched atop a hill outside of the city walls. Before lying down to a restless night of fearful dreams, he savagely hurled all of his most prized, plundered spoils from countless campaigns out from his tent with a tremendous clang. All such treasure rolled down the hill, yet come morning, none of it was to be found.

- *The Adventures of Fredrigo Benetesta: "The Libretto Omnium"* -

- Chapter V: Ira -

The lull of the following afternoon, the fifth of Easter, was disrupted by the hollow clopping of a single set of hooves upon the cobblestone road. Atop a noble steed of silken white rode a messenger from the nearby land of Rinascere, who was in search of the Count. Upon alighting from the magnificent stallion at the front gates, there was an uncanny resemblance between the man and his mount, for both were fair with long manes, which shown blonde in the sun, and were towering in stature. Thus, he burst into the great feasting hall.

He strode toward the Count who was reclining within his throne of chiseled stone, surrounded by his closest company and Fredrigo. At once the impressive foreigner spoke with a voice which deeply filled the hall.

"Gianfrancesco, lord over San Gimignano, the king of Rinascere extends to you this message of grave importance."

"I know what land from whence you hail sir," bitterly remarked the Count, who had seen far too many of the messenger's breed throughout his years. Rage flared behind his eyes upon merely gazing upon such a man. "Swiftly relay your message, before I expel you from these halls."

Without delay the man produced from his lengthy robes, whiter than purest seafoam, a scroll sealed with the mark of his King. He slowly unrolled the parchment within his broad hands and began to read:

"I, Fortinbras, King of Rinascere, hereby demand that all citizens and men of arms within the realm of San Gimignano return their stolen treasures of war from the peaceful land of Farioso at once, lest they face limitless bloodshed to come. Far too long have our nations rivaled, and I wish no harm upon you. However, if you fail to comply with such reasonable terms, I will be forced to speak the only language which you comprehend— that of clashing steel and battle. You have until the final morning sun of the Octave to do what you have been commanded, or it will be the sound of my finest legions, marching unto your walls, will wake you and your men from your sleep that fated morn and then return you to your slumber eternally."

The imposing messenger then replaced the scroll to his silken robes and awaited a response in silence. Many moments passed and the sun began to dip behind the towering walls of the city, thus casting the great hall in ever increasing darkness and shadow. The king's eyes, though, burned brighter like torch fire. At last, he spoke with the booming voice of an enraged god.

- The Adventures of Fredrigo Benetesta: "The Libretto Omnium"-

"Return what has been stolen? This is madness!" said he while slowly rising from his throne. "Why shall I reward their weakness? They were but babes amid these cruel realms and such was their destiny."

"My lord, perhaps we might—"

"Silence Fredrigo! Do not mettle with such stately affairs. You know not the needs of my people." The Count's complexion began to swell with boiling blood and fury. "You, sir messenger, dare to come into my halls and demand our submission and apology? You shall receive neither!" The Count strode toward the man bathed in white and towered over him, though the messenger was far taller. "You will have nothing to return to your precious lands with, nor will you even make the journey." His meaty fingers clenched around the messenger's thin neck of sleek flesh, squeezing tighter as each labored breath left the man's lungs.

"Stop at once!" pleaded the man. "No Count of high class threatens a messenger," he managed to spurt out in between gasps for life.

"Only in the halls of hell might you come before me again." Like a savage animal, the Count pounced upon his unwanted guest in a fit of rage. All present looked on, unmoving, in horrid silence, for no one comes between a wrathful beast and his prey. And thus, they observed their lord strangle the life out

- The Adventures of Fredrigo Benetesta: "The Libretto Omnium"-

of the messenger with one hand, as his enraged eyes ever seared into the victim's soul. Once this had been brutally done, the Count dragged the lifeless lump of flesh by the ankles and savagely flung the richly robed warm body into the blazing hearth at the opposite end of the hall. Shouts of the Count's fury filled the night and still reverberate deep within the castle walls.

  The Count now sat in silence as he maliciously looked upon the melting flesh within the flames. Soon the once impressive man of grand stature would be indistinguishable among the logs and ash. Legend tells of the wrath of Achilles, and never before until this moment had such mythological fury been challenged. As all others remained petrified out of fear, none but Fredrigo firmly strode towards the ever-fuming Count.

  "'Man has no greater enemy than himself.' Such were the poetic words of Petrarch of Arezzo," said he hardheartedly to the Count. "And you would do well to learn such verse, than to remain in your savagery. Arise at once, your many guests will soon be among you, but I fear you have far to come and your days are now numbered." The Count's enflamed ears turned white with heat, yet he restrained himself from slaying the scholar where he stood, for in that moment, the doors were thrown open and the night's guests began pouring into the freshly sullied hall, now permeating with the smell of roasting flesh.

- The Adventures of Fredrigo Benetesta: "The Libretto Omnium"-

The ashes of the cremating corpse hovered in the air throughout the evening. Warriors and women alike deeply feared what was to come to their gates at the last sunrise of Easter. For indeed, the count in his irrational rage condemned the souls of a vast host of his people. Now they could only wait on what tragic fate lied before them. All present attempted to forget their impending woes at the bottom of many cups of mead, yet with no success. The Count himself remained within his fit of fury, thus leaving impressions of his fingertips upon each chalice of soft gold he clutched and grinding through each chicken bone to meet his teeth. All throughout the night he sipped on bitter wine. He spoke to no one, and his hateful eyes ensured that no one would come within his mighty arm's swing. However, there was always one who never regarded such repulsive mannerisms. Tonight, it was Fredrigo who requested that they retire, at once, to the crypt for the night's reading, before any more brave men became kindling for the hearth. The Count begrudgingly complied; however, none from the usual company deemed it safe to join, as they saw the glow still radiating from their fuming lord. Suddenly overcome by illness or overbearing drowsiness, the Count's retinue scurried off to bed, fearing that they would not see Fredrigo again come morning.

And thus Fredrigo and the Count descended unaccompanied into the crypt, which housed riches destined to outlast the end of time, though all seemed insignificant within the

Count's gradually altering heart. Returning to the text, Fredrigo resumed conveying such eternal wisdom, which had once been locked away for centuries.

*   *   *   *   *

XXXI Octobris MCVI Anno Domini

My Lord called out to me along my journey, telling me to go forth from the cavern of forsaken darkness and search for the land of perpetual sunshine—a place where the skies ever burn, and the rains never come. For months on end I traveled countless realms in search of this hidden land of legend; and yet, no matter where I trekked, the sun always slipped away, giving rise to the hallow moon of early evening, proving that I was as far away as ever.

I then traveled west into the boundless desert of which none have returned. As I traversed innumerable mountains and valleys of the driest, course sand, the days grew longer, and the night stayed only but for an hour. Thus, I continued on through the suffocating sandstorms, never looking back for days on end, for I knew I was close. My water had long been spent, and yet I trudged on beneath torrid glare and relentless winds, never planning to return until my purpose had been fulfilled.

The hours slipped away like fine sand between the fingers. My tongue ran dry and tasted of sea salt, as my throat begged for all else but more swallowed sand. The rest of my aching body had become desert blasted by the abrasive gusts, and my windblown hair and lashes harbored enough grinded silt to fill a shallow grave. My lips withered to the same faded pale hew of my cheeks and crackled like a decade dried riverbed. And yet never did I stop or rest, for each night, the stars shown for a shorter span.

On the fortieth day, I was all but vanquished by the heat and drought. Soon, I too would blow away in the wind. Summoning all the strength deep within my dried bones, I crawled atop the highest dune within sight. For hours I ascended the mount of sand in agony. The blistering sun scorched ever hotter as I slowly climbed towards her. At last, I clawed through the course sand atop the dune and collapsed with closed eyes glaring into the relentless blaze above. I had only the strength to turn my head, but what was seen only disparaged me further. There was no city. Only the indistinguishable mounds of sand stretched in every direction. There I lay outstretched, and as the temporary night fell, two tears mixed to mud trickled from my eye lids. Doubting anger soon filled my heart. Forsaken and in failure, I drifted away, like the final waning grains in an hour glass.

When I woke, the sun had softened and the winds had ceased. Out of the corner of my feverish eye, I saw what appeared to be a small pool glistening from the sun's gleam.

- The Adventures of Fredrigo Benetesta: "The Libretto Omnium"-

Alongside the shallow pool, which glittered like glass amid the sand, rose a short tree with broad palms. Each thread within my thirsting flesh drew me towards this oasis of mortal deliverance. I began to stumble down the mount, refusing to blink lest my eyes lose what had been so desperately found. I collapsed once more at the base of the dune, as my body could no longer withstand my own weight. Yet unswerving in my demands for survival, I began to drag my body facedown through the desert, tilling the sand with my fingers as I went, until at last my outstretched hand splashed in the revitalizing waters of divine intervention.

I lifted palm after palm of water to my face, as such soothing liquid dripped from my cheeks and seeped through the sand. Each drop renewed the hope within my soul, for, indeed, I had not been forsaken. After my shriveling throat had been replenished, I pulled my body toward the water and slipped into the shallow pool. Lightly drifting beneath the waters for quite some time, I felt each wilted muscle revive within the healing pool, and I sprang forth out of the water, born anew.

'Drink deeply,' whispered a compassionate voice, 'for, indeed, you have traveled quite a ways.'

Startled, I brushed aside the wet hair before my eyes, unveiling a woman draped in the light blue tones of an early spring's sky. She cupped her hands together and smiled sweetly in silence. Despite the harsh, gritty winds, her brown hair was

- The Adventures of Fredrigo Benetesta: "The Libretto Omnium"-

soft and shimmered in the sun. Nothing about her was threatening in the slightest, as she waited upon me, patiently.

'Maiden, who are you? And where have I come? I am sorry, for in my refreshing bliss, you must have gone unseen.'

'I am the one they call Pazenza, though it is not my given name.' She spoke leisurely, as if by calming song. I remained in the water, as she, standing close along the bank, continued, and 'You have come to nowhere, as nothing but wind and swirling sand roam these lands for hundreds of miles. Why have you wandered so deep within this barren realm? Nothing awaits you here.'

Drying my dripping eyes and cheeks against my fingers, I said, 'I have been sent to find the land, where the sun never sets and the rain never comes. I thought myself abandoned, but now that I have found redemption within this place, I know myself to be along the righteous path.'

'A place of everlasting sunshine? Has your thirst brought you to madness? Surly no such place exists.' He voice quivered as she spoke.

'No, I know it to be true. Never before has my master led me astray. No longer shall I rest until I come upon that place.' The woman was now shaking visibly, as I stepped out of the pool. I placed a hand upon her shoulder, looking deep into her troubled eyes. 'And you know where it is…don't you?'

Hey eyes slipped from mine and peered toward the ground. 'I knew it well; it was my home.' She shivered as the memories of a frightful past seemed to well within her heart. 'That place is now a wasteland, ravaged by wrath. Nothing awaits you there.'

'It is my calling,' said I while slowly raising her downturned glance back towards mine. 'Will you not help me?'

She exhaled deeply. Pausing for a moment, she then spoke, 'I will lead you to my homeland to fulfill your calling, but you must save my people.'

'If it is willed, then so shall it be.'

After filling our water skins and plucking some fresh fruit from the budding tree, we set out toward the land of her patrimony—the realm of everlasting heat. We trekked throughout the scalding sand for what seemed like many days on end, though telling the passage of time became difficult as the night began to gradually melt away.

At last, the mounds of sand began to give way to parched spans of flattened, crackled ground. There, we came upon the brim of a vast canyon, scratching deep into the earth and extending leagues in length. Oceans could be poured within such a broad fissure without any overflow. If God were to crack the world open like an egg, such a canyon would be the result.

'Look down into the crevice and see what has become of my nation.'

The fissure was so deep, that only by placing my toes along the crumbling edge could I directly see to the bottom. At once, a surge of angered voice rushing up the steep walls engulfed my ears. There were war cries, oaths of hatred, and sounds of clashing battle. Such raging tones echoed off the canyon walls and distorted my perception, thus it was incredibly difficult to see the buzzing scene beneath me. At last, after much struggle, the graphic scene below came into focus.

There was wailing and gnashing of teeth. Within the forsaken canyon, hordes of men and some women were locked in grueling warfare. Bodies were indistinguishable amid clouds of dust, severed flesh, and gleaming steel. The canyon floor was completely unseen as the host densely flowed both directions in raging anarchy. There were buildings, now crumbled in ruin, diverting the stream of battle like a river coursing around a stone.

'These are my people. When the war ignited over petty, long forgotten matters, I climbed out of this savage crevice and sought refuge. Such happened decades ago, and yet their wrathful hearts still clash in battle. They fight no longer for cause or banner. Now each man has abandoned all loyalty. They clash in

- The Adventures of Fredrigo Benetesta: "The Libretto Omnium"-

one direction for days on end until they reach the far end of the canyon; there each warrior turn around to battle against the same men who had been fighting for the same cause behind them. A nation is at constant war. Never do they stop to rest, for the sun never sets, and gradually the canyon floor rises as each generation fights upon the slain remains of their forefathers.'

'What a truly horrid land,' said I, slowly backing away from the edge. 'Never do I wish to enter such a throng.'

'But it is your life's calling…your *vocation*. You must save these men, as they know not what they do, for they know no better.'

'Never shall I—' just then the howling desert wind picked up once more. With a sudden blast of heated air, I was thrown over the rocky brim and directly into the raging carnage of battle.

I crashed upon the crude helmets of two men beating one another with clubs. They fell lifeless upon the heap, and I was badly wounded from the fall. My moans were drowned in the endless clamor of clashing metal and rally cries. The place reeked of rotting flesh in the hellfire sun. I was relentlessly pummeled like being trampled by a heard of stampeding beasts. Rolling over to avoid a falling mace, I found myself gazing into the decaying face of a freshly slain man. His eyes were young, yet dimmed and hollow, and a festering wound plagued his neck. Startled, I pushed off the carnal ground to stand amid the chaos.

At once, I was smacked, slashed, and beaten from all sides. I crouched my body to shield my face and chest, yet the blows ever fell upon me. With each biting strike, I felt the rage swelling within my heart beneath the blazing sun. I craved nothing more than to draw my blade and slay all within my sight. I could have done so, for I knew my strength. With each pound upon my flesh, the wrath further swelled. Soon the canyon would be brimming with the blood of the fallen nation before me.

I threw out my arms wide, thrusting a dozen men back upon each other, and reached for my sacred sword. Yet as I drew the blade, I looked toward the heavens to behold a terrifying sight. The sun's gleam had been blocked by the steep fissure bank which had begun to close. Less heat entered the canyon by the second as the massive crack within the Earth began to seal. Within the hour, all would be entombed inside the raging canyon eternally with sword in hand, among the dead.

At once, I raised my palms into the air releasing the firmly clenched blade from my unbloodied hands, and shouted with a God-like voice which was not my own:

'*PEACE!* Let there be peace among you!' The storm calmed immediately, and for the first time in decades, the cave fell silent. 'Look to the sky!'

In unison, all those bloodied and battered stared upon terror at the fate which awaited them. Never before had these men witnessed such happenings, for they were always locked in battle and thus had never shifted their gaze toward the heavens since war began to ravage the land. As the canyon continued to squeeze at a slow, yet visibly tormenting rate, every blade and club alike shattered upon the ground of flesh and steel, leaving each fury-ridden man defenseless, yet with two able, empty hands.

'Your weapons!' yelled I, echoing to every living soul within the closing canyon. 'Men, shed your arms, armor, and shields and heap them together as one, so that we may ascend such a mound of our discarded weapons of war to our living freedom.'

Without exception, the vast host of thousands threw their clubs, swords, maces, and shields atop the growing mound, as the sun began to disappear through the shutting ceiling. All was soon almost in total shadow. Scampering up the mount of surrendered armaments, the once raging host ascended to safety, where Pazenza awaited them. I climbed last and in darkness, as the sun was all but sealed away. The crevice which had once been a league in width, only had an arm's length in breadth when I came to the peak of the assembled mound. And yet, I was still rather far beneath the rapidly converging edge to the surface. The sun was all but gone and the canyon walls began to compress my nose, when, at last, I jumped like an ancient Greek Olympian, barely snagging the edge by three fingers. At once, I was grabbed

- The Adventures of Fredrigo Benetesta: "The Libretto Omnium"-

by many men and pulled through the closing sliver that had once been a breath-taking chasm. Scarcely had we all survived such an escape; and yet, had all but one man retained his shield, all would have perished a tortuous death.

'You have saved my people!' beamed Pazenza, who had seen all from above. 'I owe you my life and all that is mine.'

'No dear lady, it is they who have saved me. Go now and start a new, peaceful nation with your beloved and cleansed kin. I must go now to pursue my own journeys toward unthinkable treasure, of which I slowly approach the end.

* * * * *

The scholar returned the crumbling, ancient text atop the pedestal without speaking.

"Fredrigo..." said the Count with a sigh, "I dread my hateful actions may have endangered my people. I knew no better than my militant ways, and now I live in fearful regret. I humbly ask that you stay within the walls for the next couple of days in order to advise me through these impending trials. With you here, this realm and my people a have brighter hope for what is to come. And though your readings keep my eyes thoroughly awake each night, come morning, I am fortified as a better man, like iron melted down and forged into steel. Though I know not what will await us come the next two sunrises, there is one constant which ever rings true in my mind—all within these lands need you here now, in our most pressing times. I feel it destined that you came to these gates."

"Men may choose their destiny, but grand design is inescapable. I shall remain here as you wish, Francesco. Let us get some rest. Though I see not what lies ahead either, your people will undoubtedly be in grave need of you in the upcoming hours. I bid you goodnight fair Count."

That evening it was Fredrigo who lay awake—his mind swirling as he tried to figure out how to save the people and the lord of San Gimignano.

- *The Adventures of Fredrigo Benetesta: "The Libretto Omnium"*-

- Chapter VI: Invidia -

The following morn, all arose in silent sorrow. It was the penultimate day of Easter, and yet every soul knew and drearily awaited what was to be upon them come the next sunrise. This was the last innocent daybreak of the Octave, for tomorrow, the red sun is destined to rise above the walls, bathing all in scarlet and crimson.

The sleepless scholar gingerly stepped down the winding staircase and came upon the Count and General Forza seated at table, discussing defensive preparations for the impending clash on the upcoming horizon.

"Our catapults will hurl enough great boulders upon them to rumble the earth on which they stand, and should they attempt to scale our walls, vast cauldrons of boiling tar await them," spoke General Forza, pounding his fist upon the stone table. "My warriors are ready and grind upon axe and blade as we speak. Those who march from the whitewashed halls of Rinascere will be unable to breach our walls, and we shall slay such highbrowed scoundrels in their rich robes."

"Forza," calmly spoke the Count in a tone which sharply contrasted that of the general's, "I am pleased with your efforts, and I trust that you will do everything necessary to defend these lands and all within them. I give you leave," he said before turning toward Fredrigo, "as I now have many other matters to discuss." After the general strutted out of the room, the Count put his arm around his noble guest and said, "Come with me. There is much I need to show you."

And so he led Fredrigo through many concealed corridors and passage ways which the scholar had never before seen, until they came upon a massive stairwell, which wound like an immense python. And thus they ascended rather arduously for quite some time until they had reached a little latched wooden door at the top of the staircase. The Count threw it open, revealing an unimpaired view of the Tuscan countryside, now blooming in early spring.

"Come forth, Fredrigo. This is the tallest tower in the realm, from here all can be seen."

"And yet, I see nothing," said he while stepping out.

"Well, what do you seek to find?"

"Such is the question of life, dear Count."

"Indeed it is… Look to the East. Atop that ridge lies the city of Rinascere. When my eyes were younger, I would climb

- The Adventures of Fredrigo Benetesta: "The Libretto Omnium"-

this tower and scowl upon their domes and columns of finest stone each day. Though I no longer throw anger towards them, I deeply envy their refinement beyond all extents. My men walk around clad in freshly slain furs, while they are draped in softest silks. Their halls are crafted in the finest marbles, while ours are chiseled from shallow rock. And now they march toward our walls to slay my people." He paused for a moment and returned in a far off voice of longing, "Theirs is a kingdom I would slay any man to rule."

"You mustn't envy that of others. Such is the quickest way to the corrupted heart."

"I can no longer see within their walls, for my eyes have grown old and weary." As he dreamily spoke, he pulled out a looking glass, that of which sailors use, and gazed toward his desired gem on the fleeting horizon.

"Look not toward that city, but out to the creations of the world—the plains, lakes, rivers, and beasts. What do you see?"

"I see a forsaken land. The doves, flowers, and meadows before me all show bleak against the cold reality which is to come." Twilight had begun to roll over the horizon as the sun dipped beneath the hills. "Soon there shall be darkness, yet I fear even more what is destined come next light." Fredrigo took the looking glass from the Count and began to feel it on all sides. It

- The Adventures of Fredrigo Benetesta: "The Libretto Omnium"-

was of tarnished brass and undoubtedly stolen long ago from some other luckless land.

"You have a fine scope, my lord. There is one who hailed from Pisa, who used such instruments to find new worlds within the sky. Look unto the starry herald—the heavens and moon above and beyond. Now what do you see?"

"There are only but a few points of light amid the eternal darkness. Those which glimmer amid the black shine bright, yet soon they too shall be swallowed in shadow, for everything returns to dust and darkness. Beyond the firmament there is nothing but emptiness and the world's sorrows."

"My Count, you are blind, but soon you shall see."

Not long after, they returned to the great hall for what was to be a rather solemn night of feasting. None knew what was to come in the morning, and many feared that this eve would be their last. There was no music or dancing in the hall that night. Only the distant tune of blades being ground in the armory could be heard. Precious little was consumed by the people, as warriors painted their faces and anointed their bodies with oil for the glorious battle which awaited them. All soon returned to their dwellings for what was to be a restless night of fearful watch. And thus, all remaining solemnly processed into the crypt to hear from the ageless book of immortal wisdom. For many present, this was to be their final deliberate act upon this Earth. Fredrigo

- The Adventures of Fredrigo Benetesta: "The Libretto Omnium"-

felt the true weight of the ancient manuscript within his hands for the first time. He exhaled deeply, and then continued to read the tale which was to be above all tales—the penultimate chapter of the guide to immortality.

*   *   *   *   *

XXV Decembris MCVI Anno Domini

 I went forth from the perpetual desert, never again to return to that foul scorch. After many days, the dunes had long melted into the horizon, and I came upon a thriving forest. The feel of fresh grass beneath my feet and an herbal smell of the humid wood brought me to bliss. I soon came up to a flowing stream. It ran gently in the tranquil forest, yet was too broad to bound across. Stepping within the cool brook, I cleansed myself of all the lingering sand and blood still clinging to my flesh. Once all the remnants of a grisly past had been washed away, I sat beneath the outstretched branches of an ancient tree and slowly drifted off to destined dreams.

 Within my dreams I envisioned myself atop an enormous mountain, though I knew not where. It was not a fierce mountain with whipping winds and snowcapped peaks, but rather it was a warm mountain, which pierced through the sky and climbed toward the sun. The higher I ascended, the warmer and brighter all things became, and a pleasant breeze ever breathed life into the abounding flowers and fields upon the mountain. One day, at

- The Adventures of Fredrigo Benetesta: "The Libretto Omnium"-

the end of all eternity, I reached the peak, though what I saw atop the mount, was beyond description.

The warm sleep that had poured over my eyes slowly began to drip away, and I awoke from my vivid dream with a pleasant feeling of delight. I remained in that dreamy daze beneath the tree for quite some time, until my eyes came across something which pricked me from my drowsiness. Only but a stone's throw from where I lay, rested a small wooden raft with a paddle on the near side of the river, caught within the reeds along the shoreline. Such a vessel was not present before my slumber, but I knew not how long I was ensnared within my dreams.

I searched the thick wood far and wide to seek out the man to whom the raft belonged, but to no avail. Moreover, I seemed to be the only soul within a league, as all was pleasingly silent amid the trees save the sounds of the coursing stream and gently rustling leaves. I returned to the creek, to find the raft of fastened logs still remaining. I pulled it ashore as to prevent the streaming current from carrying her away; and yet as I did so, I came across another rather curious circumstance. Upon the handle of the wood-carved paddle, the letters 'A.S.' were deeply engraved. Though I thought it impossible, I began to ponder that perhaps the raft had been sent for me.

As I lay the simple boat back into the water, the current of the cool creek began to vigorously course around me and the water grew warm. I knew then that I was destined to travel along the flowing stream, though I knew not where it was to lead me. Thus, I began to embark upon my lengthy voyage toward the penultimate trial of my grueling quest.

 I paddled effortlessly along the coursing creek, like stroking through a blowing breeze, as I traveled within the cool shade of the tree canopy. The creek soon gave rise to broader streams and then to vast rivers, yet the guiding current remained ever constant. By the second day, the waterway lead out of the dense forest foliage, as it traveled north toward the countryside. Never was I hungry, for each morning I docked upon the mainland to gather wild berries and small game for the day's journey. Nor did I thirst, as refreshing rain showered from the heavens at the beginning of each afternoon, causing the river to swell beyond her banks. At the coming of each night fall, I rocked away to ever more peaceful dreams atop the raft, as I continued to course down the waterway, lying on my back, facing the stars. Such were my pleasant travels along the river, though my destination was to prove far less lovely.

 One fateful evening, I was jarred from my sleep by a clap of thunder and the roll of the raging current. As the heavens unleashed a surging squall upon the river, I fearfully realized that the rain-swollen stream had dragged me into roaring rapids. Amid the deluge, I reached for my lone oar, but it was of no use against the thrashing river. Each shore was many lengths away;

- The Adventures of Fredrigo Benetesta: "The Libretto Omnium"-

thus, there was no hope of finding sanctum upon land. The winds whipped from every side and stripped broad branches from ageless trees, throwing them and other debris into the once untainted water. Nothing could be seen amid the ceaseless downpour, as I coiled my hands within the rope ties of the raft, bracing myself against torrents from above and below. Webs of lightning gave the only illumination from the raging black sky. Drenched to the core, all sight and touch had long been washed away, yet it is what I soon heard which enkindled fear in my soul.

There was a distinct rushing echo, resounding above the thunderous vibration of the rapids and storm. A flash of lighting lit up the air for half a moment, and I caught brief glimpse of my rapidly approaching undoing, yet such a foretaste was far long enough. The fated current, which had guided me thus far along the once pleasant river, was soon to come to an abrupt end, for the great falls were before me. I paddled in a frantic fury against the current, yet such efforts were like an inescapably hooked fish flailing for its life against the line of a heartless fisherman. I reached for the large boulders standing fast against the river, but the incessant rains from on high made everything too slick to grasp. The falls were now upon me, nothing could be done to avoid this accursed fate. With a pulsing heart, I crested the apex and began my freefall, as one final bolt lit up the sky.

A distant rumble of the fleeting storm awoke me from my swoon. I was washed up amid the muck of the riverbank, caked

- The Adventures of Fredrigo Benetesta: "The Libretto Omnium"-

in unknown filth. I knew not how far I had been lifelessly dragged by the unforgiving river, but no longer could I hear the roar of the falls and the lightning flashes waned in the distance. The rain had slowed to a drizzle, and I began to shiver amid the darkness. Just then, I saw the light of a faint lamp, beyond the tree line, and the silhouette of a small cottage. I began to stagger towards the light, scrapping off the globs of mud as I walked.

Upon the first knock, an elderly woman in an apron unlatched her door with a sweet smile. At once, she seemed dismayed at the sight of me, but such was out of caring concern.

'My dear, what has happened to you? Come… come in at once.'

I crossed the threshold of her single-roomed cottage and was at once filled with life afresh due to the rich aromas of sweet breads which permeated throughout her dwelling. My cheeks and flesh were well warmed by the wood burning oven, which kept the place thoroughly heated.

'My lady, I thank you for welcoming me into your warm home. I am Azrael. I was caught within the rapids and thrown over the falls.'

'Azrael…' she whispered to herself while pondering. Then she spoke softly, 'Many young men have begun to tell of your legend and adventures all throughout the land.' She giggled.

'Here, give me your dripping robes, and I shall place them by the stove to dry. You can call me Dolcezza. Do you hunger at all my dear?'

'I give you thanks my lady. Yet, what do you mean? How do others and you know of me and my works?'

'Oh it matters not dear. Are you certain you desire nothing to eat?' she pestered.

'I am sure,' said I in growing frustration, but then I looked into her kind eyes and the wrinkles upon her face and hands. Beneath her loving smile was a woman who had seen much in her years and knew much more. My anger softened as her lips slowly spread from worn cheek to cheek.

'Tell me child…' her voice rang like that of a kind mother, 'what are you searching for along your quest?'

Unexpecting of such a question, it took many moments to gather my thoughts. 'I cannot explain what I seek, for I do not truly know. It is an eternal treasure of great price, far above any worldly gem—an immortality without pain or suffering beyond comprehension. Yet even more, it is an existence in redemptive bliss for all eternity. Such is what I seek.'

She smiled one last time. 'Then why do you linger here? Your clothes are dry. Go now to fulfill you quest.' She squeezed my hands and gazed proudly into my eyes. 'I shall pack you some food for your travels.'

And so I set out once again to follow the river in the dead of night. With my raft long since swallowed by the falls, I walked along the bank of the coiling river, which wound throughout the land like a serpent. The banks became muddier with each step as the trees and surrounding lands grew ever more swampy. The air was foul and humid, as hundreds of bugs chirped in the moonlight. Moss clung to every branch and trunk. Daring not to sleep in such a foul and eerie land, I trudged on all through the night.

The following sunrise was hidden behind a quilt of clouds covering every inch of the firmament. Thus, the land was cast in dreary grey shadow. Soon after, I came upon the ultimate end of the great river. After miles of winding through woodlands, countryside, and cascading over falls, the stream emptied into a massive marsh. Scummy water stretched beyond measure and was only interrupted by patches of long reed grass, stemming through the water. Insects of all kinds buzzed about and the air hung with the muggy scent of herbal decay. A forbidding fog hovered over the water, concealing the terrors of the swamp.

I began to wade through the wetland. The water was warm, but festering with unseen creatures. And though the marsh only rose toward my lower thigh, it was so dense and dirty that

- The Adventures of Fredrigo Benetesta: "The Libretto Omnium"-

my feet had completely disappeared within the water. The swamp bed was sludgy and slipped beneath me with each step, and a nauseating vapor seemed to rise off the water, directly pervading my nostrils. I continued on, deeper into the marshlands, until something snatched my ankle.

    I thrusted my leg upward, yet the unseen beast held fast. Thrashing atop the water, I sent ripples all throughout the otherwise stagnant bog. When I could not liberate myself from such a fell clutch, I drew my blade and plunged it blindly into the murky muck. At once, the hold upon my ankle gently released. Soon after I saw the striking green eyes of the felled beast, which once held me fast. As its lifeless body rose to the surface, I appallingly saw that it was man.

    I cradled the head and shoulders of my slain victim. He was human in form, yet not in essence. His forked tongue stretched over sharpened teeth and cold lips. There was no hair upon his pale flesh, and he seemed to ooze a thick mucus from every pour. His nails came to razor tips like his teeth, and his bulging blue veins cut throughout his body in the shape of diamonds, giving the subdermal impression of scales. Yet the most shocking of his features, were the raging green eyes which burned ever more vividly in death. Such was the fate of a man possessed by some sinful sickness.

- The Adventures of Fredrigo Benetesta: "The Libretto Omnium"-

I pitifully let his head dip back into the water and continued on. Yet only had I taken three steps more, before I was violently snatched again, and then once more! The sludgy water all about me soon lit up with hundreds of eerie green eyes. Like a frenzied beast, I thrashed fiercely to liberate myself, yet more and more hooked hands latched on. They savagely tore at my robes and yanked upon my sheathed blade, yet above all else they dragged upon my shoulders and slashed at my submerged legs, forcing me to topple into the murky water in which all things vanish.

Nothing could be heard beneath the sludgy swamp water, not even shouts of agony. Their teeth began to slice into my flesh, and amid my raging struggles, I was in dire need of air. Death was upon me. Yet in an ultimate surge of gifted strength, I tore free of claw and fang and burst through the surface.

Rushing through the thigh deep bog, my lungs struggled to fill with the muggy air, as the green-eyed host viciously pursued me. I raced deep into the swamp, heaving in the humid air with each stride, until I entered a region of darker fog which stung my eyes. Those in chase shockingly halted at once, daring not to enter such a realm. And thus, for only but a moment, I could catch my breath in safety, completely unaware of what lurked within the darkened fog.

I was lost amid the thick haze. Wandering to find my way out, I only cut deeper into the darkness. The fog was so dense that I could no longer see the fingertips of my outstretched arm in every direction. Then I heard a malicious laugh which resonated in my soul and chilled my blood. I could not perceive from where it came, as the deep snicker echoed and seemed to swirl around me. I wheeled around, yet could see nothing. My heart throbbed against the inside of my ribs.

'Are you lossssst Azzzreal?' I heard the soul's wrenching laugh anew, yet this time an immense set of radiating emerald eyes burned through the fog to meet me, then rose high above the water. At once, the blinding haze about me was lifted, unveiling a slithering serpent of biblical proportions.

Broad scales the size of chariot wheels surrounded me on all sides. As I had wandered amid the blinding fog, this coiling beast had wrapped a wide circular perimeter about me many times over. I was imprisoned within a colosseum of reptilian skin, and rising above it all was the hissing archetype of evil. Each dripping fang would have dwarfed a mammoth tusk and its forked tongue snapped like a pronged whip. Its sleek eyes glowed green like fallen stars. Never before had such terror pumped through my veins.

'How—how is it that you speak?' shouted I, attempting to hide my fear, though it seeped from every word.

- The Adventures of Fredrigo Benetesta: "The Libretto Omnium"-

'I speak to all men,' said he with a cruel laugh, 'beginning with your forefather, Adam.'

I was trembling now, as he began to slither about me. There was a sickening aura about him which drained me of all courage. 'Then it was you, who was banished from the garden of paradise?' said I, while feebly drawing my sword.

'Why yesssss. Do you not wish to know all things? To create all things? To be...' he hissed in my ear, '...*immortal*?'

'Keep away from me, spawn of Satan,' firmly said I, pointing my quivering sword toward him.

'You have chosen a mortal life, suffering, and death,' he said, slowly rising high above me, 'and I shall make it so.'

He struck down upon me with brandished fangs. Driving off to the side, I nearly avoided being skewered upon such immense daggers. His neck coiled back immediately, as he snapped once more towards me. I swung my sword as to beat him back, yet it glanced against his striking fangs and threw my blade from my hand. He ferociously came once more, pinning me against a large boulder jutting out of the swamp. One of his curled teeth plunged deeply into the rock, while the other pierced through my shoulder. I howled in agony as my flesh was pumped with mortal venom. He pulled back from the rock, and laughed once more, as I staggered about, desperately searching amid the

- The Adventures of Fredrigo Benetesta: "The Libretto Omnium"-

murky water for my blade. Clutching my shoulder in anguish, I saw, at last, my glimmering steel lodged between two scales of the coiled serpent's tail.

'Why do you fight me? I could make you like a god.' And with that, he slowly cocked his neck to deliver his mighty finishing blow. In that moment, I wrenched my sword free from his scaly armor and dove aside once more. And thus the razor fangs struck where I once stood, thrusting deep into the serpent's own slithering flesh. He writhed all about, yet it only drove his dripping daggers deeper. I rose slowly, destined sword in hand. The wriggling beast was inescapably lodged within himself, yet it was I who was to bring an end to his agony and send such a vile viper back to the hell from whence it came.

'I do not envy God.' I raised my glistening blade over my head, then mercilessly brought it down upon the satanic serpent, severing head from coiled flesh. Black blood dripped to the hilt, indelibly tainting everything which it touched, and the once radiating green eyes within the beast's detached skull dimmed to gray. The serpent which had brought about the fall of man had now been vanquished, yet his spirit lives on.

At once, the sun glow from on high shown through the cloud cover and burned away the lingering fog. All was bright and gleaming. The corpse of the demonic serpent soon ignited in

- The Adventures of Fredrigo Benetesta: "The Libretto Omnium"-

a consuming, ashless blaze. Within seconds, all remnants of that immense snake vanished.

I could feel the viper's toxin slowly course towards my heart. My flesh flamed from within due to such incurable poison. I buckled at the knees, struggling to stay calm, for I knew that each fearful heartbeat drew the venom closer to my undoing. I heaved and trembled irrepressibly, as my hands and fingers began to turn blue. I looked up toward the sky and let my sword fall. The light was blinding and grew in brilliance until everything was drowned in warm, absolute radiance.

*   *   *   *   *

When Fredrigo had finished speaking all was silent. One by one they processed out of the crypt toward their beds, though no sleep was destined to relieve any of their dreary eyes. The Count remained, ensnared in a solemn trance. The scholar was last to leave and began ascending the stone steps until he heard his name.

"Fredrigo!" He turned round toward the Count, who was bent over the ancient text, which had been left open. A lone tear streaked from his once green tinged eyes, now faded blue, and splashed upon the disintegrating manuscript pages. He called out again, yet this time, gently. "Fredrigo… pray for me."

- The Adventures of Fredrigo Benetesta: "The Libretto Omnium"-

The scholarly man stared deeply into the sinner's soul and then nodded—returning, at once, to his room for the last time.

- *The Adventures of Fredrigo Benetesta: "The Libretto Omnium"*-

- Chapter VII: Superbia -

The approaching legions of Rinascere shown black against the rising red sun, which blazed behind them. They marched as one, shaking the Earth at a constant tempo like the beating of a drum. Rank upon rank of polished plate armor gleamed in the daybreak light as broad banners flew high above the masses. Armed with straight blades of steel, the vast host came upon the steep slopes leading toward the once impenetrable walls of San Gimignano.

Within such walls, the savage warriors of the estate began to gather. Slathered with pigments of war, their mighty flesh was barren, save the freshly slain hides of bears, hogs, and lions draped over their shoulders. They clenched clubs, broad axes, and war hammers within their meaty paws. Their eyes shown wide with unslaked thirst for battle, yet soon, all would drown in blood.

A stone shattering blast came forth from the base of the city slopes, as hundreds of brass molded horns sounded from the oncoming army. Then the host of clean-shaven soldiers halted steadfast at the bottom of the hill. Atop a rising tower, the Count and scholar witnessed all that was to come.

"What is the means of such horn blast?" queried Fredrigo.

"They halt to demand our submission once more," scoffed the Count. "Oh how they will wish for an end as sweet as that." He pounded the guard wall of the tower, removing a fist full of stone. "Never shall the men of these halls fall at the feet of these haughty scoundrels. Nay, I should rather die ten thousand deaths by my own hand, than to succumb to such an end."

"My lord, they march like claps of quaking thunder. We are outnumbered beyond all hope. Why do you force such fate upon your people?"

He stoically stared through the pale eyes of Fredrigo, then spoke decisively, "If it is we who dine in the halls of hell tonight, then it is they who shall serve us."

He then lifted his own battle horn of hollowed elephant tusk to his lips and blew it with the might unmatched by any mortal man. The lowly reverberating bellow sounded for leagues in each direction, signaling all within the walls to rain down upon the enemy. As the horn burst asunder from such a blast, many blazing boulders were catapulted upon the invading legions.

The projectiles smashed into the Rinascerian front lines and rolled ranks deep to the devastation of dozens. Like a

- The Adventures of Fredrigo Benetesta: "The Libretto Omnium"-

provoked viper, the army struck toward the city ramparts. The rally cry of thousands roared unendingly throughout the air, as they stormed the gates with ladders and rams. With gnashed teeth, the bearded multitude willingly awaited the swarm, for they were ready.

Atop the walls, Froza ordered wave upon wave of catapult fire. All throughout the morn, great boulders rapidly rolled down the slopes, smashing through the onslaught of invaders, yet the storm upon the gates ever raged.

The hill leading toward the estate soon flowed on all sides with boiling tar and blood. Then, the foreign legions blotted the sun with a shower of crossbow bolts, felling many men behind the walls. The cobblestone streets of San Gimignano were now studded with upright arrows lodged between the laid stones, and many civil beasts and men alike, were now skewered to the streets they once roamed. Muddied blood now coursed on both sides of the walls, and the savage cries of war soon gave rise to excruciating wails of anguish and death. But then, there was a lull in the epic clash.

"Why has the clatter of drum, shield, and battle horn all but ceased below, my Count?" asked Fredrigo, rather confounded.

"They wish no further blood to be spilled this night," said the Count somberly. "Soon they shall return to their lands to bury

- The Adventures of Fredrigo Benetesta: "The Libretto Omnium"-

their dead, and I wish it to be soon, for now we have our own freshly slain to tend."

"Such is the cost, dear Count..."

"Wait but a moment...do my eyes deceive me beyond these walls?" exclaimed the Count.

"At such a length, my sight fails me, good sir."

"They hoist up great white tents and enkindle large fires. They unload much meat from large wagons and stick their flag and war banners into the soil of my lands." With each word he grew in anger, as his cheeks swelled to a prideful crimson. "Never shall these halls be placed beneath siege, nor shall I ever remain confined within these walls like a coward, as my streets run with blood, and my people slowly starve."

"Perhaps—"

"Ney! Nevermore shall I take the counsel of scholars, Fredrigo." He was now irrepressibly trembling from the broiling conceit within his heart. In a booming voice, he spoke, "No longer shall I vainly remain here, while they feast upon my lands, dishonor these halls, and await our pathetic pleas for mercy. No... We shall ride out to meet them and christen the outskirts of San Gimignano with their blood this night. And I, Gianfrancesco, undisputed Count of this realm, shall lead the charge to triumphant victory." At once, he threw aside the tower door and began rushing down the stairs calling for General Forza to prepare his war horse.

The armies of San Gimignano amassed behind the iron-barred gates of the city. Clad in crude metals, the Count rested upon the broad back of a black stallion. Its mane was horribly entangled and its eyes were ravenous, yet there was no greater war mount. The horse's snorts were only to be outdone by the barbaric grunts of the battle-hungry horde which had assembled.

"Raise the gates!"

The Count's demand was at once met with the rattle of coiling chains. As the iron gates of the city slowly began to rise, so too did the enthralling anticipation of battle within the seething hearts of each warrior. At last, the gates had cleared, and the Count led his final glorious charge upon horseback. His men, following closely on foot, reignited their savage war cry, which could be heard all through the realm, as the mighty host surged down the slopes toward their encamped enemy.

Atop the outlook tower, Fredrigo remained ever observant. As the rumble of the thunderous charge overtook his ears, he slowly shook his head, whispering to himself, "Go therefore, most excellent disciples of folly." He turned his back toward the impending clash and began to gingerly descend the tower staircase.

- The Adventures of Fredrigo Benetesta: "The Libretto Omnium"-

The wild horde ravaged the first line of enemy camps and torched their white-tarped tents. Like an unrestrained stampede, the band of battle-entranced warriors continued to roll over rank upon rank of unprepared soldiers; however, many of the vast, foreign legions remained untouched, and thus readied themselves to push back the onslaught of raging barbarians.

The Count slew many atop his ignoble steed, and within moments, his chained mace which had once been crude, black metal, was now stained crimson. Indeed, many which had once borne silken-white robes now lay mutilated in red. Thus the Count continued to rally his men and mercilessly break his oppressors, until a stray bolt pierced his heart.

Dark blood seeped from his chest as if the festering sins within his heart had been lanced and now poured out. He was thrown from his mount and crashed upon the flesh-stained ground. The rage of battle seemed to slow and whirl within his mind, as everything faded to faint tones of gray. He could hear only the throb of each heartbeat echoing in his ears, as more precious lifeblood spewed from his wound with each pulse. At once, Forza and his best men, who had been fighting alongside the Count, converged upon him, shielding him from any further harm. While this was being done, the great general looked up, still cradling the head of his Count, to see a legion of readied ranks marching toward them. They were woefully outnumbered and certain slaughter awaited them all without exception. At

- The Adventures of Fredrigo Benetesta: "The Libretto Omnium"-

once, he called out to his men: "Fall back to the walls! Fall back!"

And thus, the wounded warriors retreated toward the walls, though they returned far fewer in number than their original departure. The fresh ranks from Rinascere were in close pursuit, as the mighty General Forza shouldered his Count up the steep slopes. At last, the Count and his loyal general entered the estate, as the broad, iron gate came slamming down. No rest was given to those safely within the walls, for now the enemy was upon them and began tearing at the fortifications.

"Men of this land," shouted the general in a broken voice, "defend your lives and homes! And pray that tomorrow we all may live in a kingdom of peace. Fear not for the Count, for I bring him now to ultimate healing. Tonight we shall all feast once more, yet unlike ever before."

And thus, he carried the fading Count down into the crypt, where Fredrigo was already awaiting them. They were accompanied by the Count's closest court who had taken refuge within this place when the battle began. They laid him on mat beside Fredrigo, surrounded by candles. And thus, for the ultimate time, the honored scholar took up the ancient *Libretto Omnium* and read forth the final enclosed secret to life eternal.

* * * * *

- The Adventures of Fredrigo Benetesta: "The Libretto Omnium"-

Far along my journey, I came to myself in a dark wood. How I came there I do not know, for I was so full of sleep and suffering, though never did I forsake the one true way. Out of that valley, I reached the base of a measureless mountain, which struck fear in my heart. The only light was that of a distant star faintly shining through the quilted cloud cover. Beckoned toward such an everlasting beacon, my soul grew restless unlike ever before. And thus, I began my ascent toward the starlit heavens and beyond—the last of my sacred trials.

I climbed all throughout the day, though in such a land there was no passage of time. All remained in shadow beneath the clouds, save the ever burning celestial flame overhead. The mount was insufferably steep, for each step I took forth was far above the previous foothold. As I neared the misty layer of clouds, an icy wind blew across me, which I had felt only once before. Such a glacial breeze bit my cheeks and chilled my nose. I threw up my hood against the cold and staggered through the wind, until the growl of a wild beast iced my blood and froze my flesh entirely.

My eyes fell upon the gnarling teeth of a lowly growling leopard. Its eyes reflected the faint starlight, and the speckled spots along its fur could only be seen for they were darker than the blackness which encompassed them. Its shiny coat and gently swaying tail appeared soft, yet never did the beast's fierce glare stray from the fresh, trembling meat it beheld.

- The Adventures of Fredrigo Benetesta: "The Libretto Omnium"-

The leopard stood atop an abandoned pile of tarnished marble, resting its padded paws upon the fractured face of what appeared to be a sculpted maiden. The icy wind blew once more. My body, paralyzed, was bound to the mountain. The pang in my shoulder flared anew, as the beast's malicious glare recalled all the suffering and woe of my past life upon my flesh once more. Crumbling beneath such torment, I fell to my knees, as the leopard cruelly descended the heap of broken stone and came forth to feast upon my sinful flesh. It was now unbearably frigid, for the chilled wind whipped ceaselessly about us, yet the beast stayed warm within its plush fleece. Though tempted, never did I look to flee, for I knew deep within that my journey was to end atop the mount, though I knew not how.

Just then, the mount began to grumble and a cascade of mud and rock rolled down from above. The rockslide crashed upon the encroaching leopard, engulfing it in the flows of sludge and rubble. Thus the beast was forever entombed, and I, unsullied by the mud, continued my ascent.

I drove my christened sword into that mount, and around such a blessed blade, I piled all that I had carried along journeys. No longer was I bound to such possessions of the earth, and my ascent was made all the less burdensome upon my soul. And so, I climbed with my eyes ever fixed upon the lone light in the heavens above.

- The Adventures of Fredrigo Benetesta: "The Libretto Omnium"-

Soon, I reached a height above the cloud cover, and as I rose out of that misty layer of dampened shade, I came upon a realm of sweet light. The faint twinkle which had shown through the dense clouds now illuminated the mountainside like the sun, yet there was no sun within the empty sky overhead, only the ever enthralling star. Thus I climbed evermore joyously, until I came upon a second beast.

The golden mane of a fierce lion came into view. The immense cat lay reclined upon a vast heap of piled gold and treasures, as it whipped its tail. Spiking out among the hoard of riches were the finest swords and armor that I have ever laid eyes upon in all my years. The lion, seeming not to have noticed my presence, yawned widely, flexing its razor-sharp front fangs. I silently tried to climb over the golden mound, for my path was entirely blocked, yet the moment my foot was placed upon the glittering trove, the beast was startled and pounced upon me in a fit of frenzied rage.

Pinned against the glimmering gold between two broad paws, I looked straight into the raving eyes of the lion. His breath smelled of hot, rotted meat. Then, the beast unleashed all of its wrath upon me in a violent roar, which reverberated throughout my soul. It echoed throughout my mind, bringing back far forgotten memories of the corrupted intellect. My tormented mind was only snapped to the present, when I saw whetted claws coming down upon me. I swiftly rolled aside, yet the beast

- The Adventures of Fredrigo Benetesta: "The Libretto Omnium"-

slashed through the back of my robes. As the lion came upon me once more with spread jaws, I snatched a blade jutting from the golden heap and drove it hilt deep within the savage beast. Thus the slain lion breathlessly lay upon me, and my plagued mind was set free.

Once I had slipped out from beneath the lifeless mane, I continued my ascent. I soon shed my slashed and tattered robes and placed them too along the mountainside. Thus I set aside the brown, hooded mantle, which I had borne for the past decade, in order to pursue even more sacred robes. I processed up the mountain in the same way I came forth into this world: naked and unbound.

As I climbed, the sky became ever brighter. My squinting eyes could hardly see, yet as I came higher, the ascent grew less difficult, for the earth far below pulled less and less upon me. The light was sweet, and as I breathed it in, my soul became ever more blissful. At last I came upon the final barrier of my lifelong journey.

Amid the light, there was one last mark of darkness upon the mount—a deprived she-wolf, frothing from the mouth. Her eyes glowed green against the bleaching white light from above. The oily fur stretched over her protruding bones gave a terribly sickly appearance, as her shriveled tongue hung limp from her open maw.

- The Adventures of Fredrigo Benetesta: "The Libretto Omnium"-

She triumphantly stood atop a mound of ravaged souls, which she had undoubtedly been feasting upon. As she raised her head to view me better, the black blood of sinful souls dripped from her stained lips. Though a vast half-eaten host lay beneath her, she hungrily eyed me with the glowing emerald stare which I had only seen once before.

The boney beast came towards me, dripping bloodied drool upon everything it passed over. I stood unflinching, for my spirit was ready. Suddenly, the she-wolf sprang upon me. In a flash of snarling teeth, fur, and slaver, I was wrestled to the ground, while the beast slowly sunk her fangs into my neck.

My soul writhed as recollections of my gravest iniquities tormented my inmost being. As the teeth plunged deeper, I slowly suffered for each of such wrongdoings of my past life. An *excruciating* pain unlike anything felt by my mortal flesh, overwhelmed my soul. As the she-beast's crushing jaw began to close and the light began to fade, I gazed up toward the ever burning beam above and spoke the final words of this life:

My Lord, into your hands I entrust my spirit, for my journey…it is finished.

Just then, the strength of all the cherubim on high flowed through me, for, indeed, my quest had not yet been fulfilled. Digging my fingers between the jagged fangs of the she-wolf, I strenuously pried apart her clenching jaws upon my neck. Once my soul had been freed, I continued to spread the beast's mouth until it cracked out of place. Thus, I threw aside the wounded wolf, never again to feast upon the troubled souls of sinful men.

And so, I ascended. Abandoning myself and the world I once knew, I climbed until everything was bathed in white. No longer could I see my moving bare feet, nor could I feel the mount beneath my toes. All was warm. I heard nothing but faint tones of the sweetest melodies. And when all melted to light, I knew my quest had been fulfilled, yet it was only the beginning of everlasting life anew.

But the journey does not end here, for death is just another bridge—one that we all must cross. Yet upon the other side, the greatest treasure above all understanding awaits for those who slay their demons. Such is the secret to immortality.

* * * * *

At last, the ancient testament of Azreal Salvestro had come to its conclusion. Upon turning the final page of the timeless manuscript, Fredrigo let the leather-bound text slip from his trembling fingers, as he could no longer bear its true weight upon his wearied soul. The ageless book fell beside the dying Count, who remained outstretched upon the stone floor, surrounded by his ever faithful retinue. Blood slowly seeped from his wounded heart, as his final moments slipped away. Without

- The Adventures of Fredrigo Benetesta: "The Libretto Omnium"-

opening his eyes, he firmly dropped a decrepit hand upon the cover of the text which had fallen beside him, then he spoke.

"Fredrigo…my dear Fredrigo…how is it that you read ink which has been so faded by age that it no longer appears on the page?" With his eyes ever sealed, the Count slowly fanned the pages of the text for all to see, revealing ancient lettering of gradually fleeting clarity. The final pages had been so worn by time that nothing but blank parchment appeared. A stupefied silence fell upon all those who had witnessed this.

All glances turned toward Fredrigo, who was calmly exhaling with his eyes closed and hands pressed together. After a moment had passed, he opened his eyes, though it made no difference, and genuinely spoke to all those present:

"Indeed, I have seen the world's beauty along my life's travels; yet now, I see nothing. Nevertheless, I am not left to journey in the darkness, for true light comes from within. I pray that one day you might all dance within such light, for once I have seen as you see, but now I look toward a higher glimmer."

Outrage soon engulfed the Count's company. "This man has gone blind! He reads not from the sacred text… He is a liar and swindler, who has abused our warmth and welcome… A fraudulent scholar stands before us! Let him be burned!"

- The Adventures of Fredrigo Benetesta: "The Libretto Omnium"-

"Peace be among you, my children," said the Count frailly, yet serenely amid his final breaths. All fell silent. His eyes remained sealed as he spoke, "You see not what Fredrigo bestowed upon you. For, indeed, he has taught us the path toward immortality, which you desire above all else, through the tailored stories of his own telling." One by one, each of the present company began to realize what had been given to them throughout these past days of the Octave. They remained in stunned silence. For the ultimate time, the Count called Fredrigo to come beside him. As the last bloody drops dripped from his suffering heart, so too did the final tears trickle toward the Count's cheeks, while he whispered his passing words in the ear of his closest friend. "Fredrigo, lead my people so that they, too, may be reborn and see anew."

In that moment, the underground crypt began to quake, for the thick walls of San Gimignano, which had once cast the realm in dark shadow came crumbling down. And thus, the light, along with the armies of Rinascere, began to pour into the city.

- The Adventures of Fredrigo Benetesta: "The Libretto Omnium"-

- *About the Author* -

Jake Berard is a 2016 graduate of Cistercian Preparatory School in Irving, Texas. This novella represents his honors senior school project. While at Cistercian, Berard was awarded the Dr. and Mrs. Claudia Mayer Memorial Award for Excellence in Humanities in addition to other awards in religious studies, English, creative writing and Latin. Jake will be entering Rhodes College in Memphis, Tennessee during the Fall of 2016 where he will study Economics, Philosophy and English with an emphasis on creative writing. In addition to writing and reading, Jake enjoys travelling, spending time with his family and flicking the disc with his little brother Jamison.

Made in the USA
Middletown, DE
11 November 2016